Rebel

A STEPBROTHER ROMANCE

KIM LINWOOD

DEDICATION

To my most incredible and much loved editor.

CONTENTS

1 ANGIE

"Come on, Angie, you've totally got this. Just talk to him!"

Cassie's grip on my arm is so tight it hurts, but she refuses to let go. Her words come a million miles per second which is a lot to handle on any regular day. Tonight, it's like dodging machine gun bullets. Vibrating with excitement, she acts like she has more at stake in this than I do, and that's saying something. My stake's pretty freaking big, after all. She yells into my ear, her voice carrying clearly over the loud dance music, "I think he's perfect."

Clubs aren't really my scene. Why blow out your eardrums when you can curl up with a good book and a cup of tea? They're so chaotic, with all the noise and lights everywhere. I mean, I'm not against going out or anything, but I don't really keep up with what's hot either, so by the time I know the songs, they're already completely last year. Dancing to music you don't know isn't nearly as much fun as it's cracked up to be.

This is such a bad idea. Only Cassie would think of something this stupidly insane and somehow manage to make it sound reasonable. I think she does it through attrition, wearing my sensibilities down until there's nothing left. It makes her too freaking persuasive for her own good. Or for mine.

But, what Cassie wants, Cassie gets. I used to try to resist, before I really got to know her, but I gave that up a long time ago. Totally not worth the trouble. She just goes ahead and does what she wants anyway.

I glance cautiously at the guy she's singled out, swallowing nervously and hoping he won't notice. He's crazy hot, like get your panties wet just at the sight hot. Wild, spiky black hair, chiseled jaw. Broad-chested and narrow-hipped, he wears a black t-shirt that looks painted onto his sculpted torso. Tall and muscled, he could've been a romance cover model. I don't see how she thinks I have a chance with him.

He can have his pick of any girl in the club, so why would he even look in my direction? I wouldn't. This is dumb.

"Cassie, I can't do this. What's Paul going to think?" There's another reason why this is a bad idea. Paul's my boyfriend. Tall, tattooed and obnoxious— in a sexy sort of way, mostly—, he's a far cry from my structured way of doing things, my carefully kept schedules and planning notebook. He's my little rebellion against my own way of life. I love that about him, or at least I like it a lot.

I know it won't last, what with me going off to college in the fall, but he's said he'll come with me and bring his motorcycle. His hog, as he calls it. I don't know, maybe it's for real. All I know is that he's really good-looking, and somehow still decided to get together with me. That puts him miles ahead of any other guy I've been interested in.

He's so far out of my league, though. Not as far as the hunk of man right in front of me, but honestly I'm just waiting for Paul to wise up and realize he's dating a dork. Cassie says he'd be an idiot if he did, but as my bff, she's supposed to say those things. What's she going to say? That I'm a nerd and our days are numbered?

Lately, he's been pushing for us to go all the way. God, listen to me. It's like I'm back in middle school. Fine, he wants to fuck me, and I've been stalling because I've never done it before. I'm terrified that he'll think I'm a prude or hate it with me since I don't know what I'm doing. So that's why I'm now a part of Cassie's Big Master Plan To Get Me Laid ™.

She stares at me with big eyes, like I'm crazy. "Paul must never know! This is for the both of you. The first time always sucks. Get it out of the way with someone you don't care about." She nods her head in the hot guy's direction. "Like him."

Someone I don't care about. If I really cared about Paul, would I have let her talk me into this at all? Wouldn't it feel more wrong? No, I do. I have to. Otherwise, what would be the point?

My gaze follows her nod, and I realize hot guy's looking right at me. Our eyes lock, and his narrow while mine go wide. Oh crap. The corners of his mouth turn up in a confident smirk that makes me tingly just as my stomach drops. If he can affect me like that from over there…

It's like he hears my thoughts. He pushes off the

wall by flexing his back and walks confidently in our direction, his gaze never wavering from mine. My voice is a panicked hiss, but while I'm whispering to Cassie, I can't tear my eyes away from him. "He's coming this way. What do I do?"

"Smile, hon." She nudges me with her elbow. "At least *try* not to look like a deer trapped in headlights."

Yeah, right. I idly play with my curls, but let go at Cassie's sharp whisper, "Stop fiddling."

He's tattooed, and not with little half-filled ones like Paul's. It wasn't so obvious from across the room, but as he comes nearer I see how they twine around his bulging biceps like inky snakes The club lights flash over him, pulling him out of the half-darkness and make the abstract designs stand out clearly. They writhe on his skin, rippling along with his muscles and crawling into his shirt. My mouth goes dry as I wonder how much of him is covered.

His deep hazel eyes roam up and down my body, and he doesn't even try to hide it. I wish I'd picked a slightly more modest dress. This one had looked good when I was fifteen, but while I'm not any taller now, my curves have filled out since then, and the difference is enough to firmly move it from *cute with a hint of sexy* to *totally painted on.*

"Don't think I didn't see you girls looking." His deep voice carries through the loud music, as arrogant as his smirk. He looks older than us, but not by a lot. Maybe twenty-three or twenty-four.

"Hi!" Cassie's pitches her voice higher than normal and pushes her ample chest out. I don't think it even occurs to her that she's doing it. It's just how she is, especially around guys she likes. "I'm Cassandra, and my shy friend here's Angie."

Yep. Shy friend. Heat rushes to my face as he studies me intently.

Still smirking, he seems to be having way too much fun. "Yeah? I'm Gavin." He speaks to both of us, but his eyes are locked on me. Why, I've no idea, with Cassie showing so much cleavage that you could rappel down between her breasts. How am I supposed to compete with that?

She looks distracted for a second, then reaches into that same cleavage and pulls out a small, pink phone. The back panel reads "SLUT" in jagged, purple letters, making me roll my eyes. Gavin arches an eyebrow. She glances up briefly and smiles before scrolling through her messages. She's totally faking it. "On vibrate," she explains, as if she's not being obvious.

Gavin and I exchange a brief glance while we wait, and then she's done. "I gotta go. I'm sorry, guys, but something's come up." She winks at me, and my gut clenches. She's leaving me here with him. Just like that? What do I do?

"Listen, Gavin, why don't you take care of Angie. Make sure she has company." It's so obviously a ruse that she doesn't even bother hiding her wide grin. "See that she gets home safe."

This is crazy. "I don't think—"

"Sure," he cuts in. "Just go do whatever it is you need to do that's not here. I'll take good care of her." His hand lands right at the small of my back and pulls me closer. It's warm, his long fingers spanning from one side of me to the other.

I look up at him, pleading with my eyes. "Listen, this is a bad idea. I'm not…" What aren't I, exactly?

"Not that kind of girl? Not up for a good time? Not going to stay up past bedtime?" He steps around to my front and puts his finger under my chin so I can't look away. "Or not going to leave me here all alone?"

I retreat without even thinking about it, until the hard wall is against my back. He stalks after me, fencing me in with his arms. Damn it, Cassie. This is too much. She threw me to the freaking wolves.

Gavin smiles, white teeth flashing. Not a wolf, a shark. "Let me guess, little girl. You're off to college soon, and…" he draws it out before he continues. "And your best friend thinks you should go take a walk on the wild side before you get there. And now she's left you with me."

I swallow past the lump in my throat. He's eerily close to the mark. "You do this a lot?"

"Babe, I can show you things you've never even known to dream about." He leans in, so close I can smell him. He's all testosterone, all masculinity. "I'm good." He trails a finger along my jaw. "I'm the best." He's also arrogant as hell.

Trying to look around his massive body, I search for Cassie, but while I'm sure she's watching gleefully someplace nearby, I don't see her. How did I let her talk me into this? God, this is crazy.

"Eyes on me, babe. I want to get lost in those gorgeous brown pools." The sheer intensity of him scares me. I can't tell how much of his interest is real, and how much is just love of the chase. "I want to see them beneath me as I slide into you."

My sex clenches in spite of my misgivings. Okay, so I want him. He's full of himself, but there's no denying he's hot. This was the plan, right? Now I just have to follow through with it.

"I guess it's your lucky night. Just like, tone down the macho a little, alright? My bullshit meter doesn't go to eleven," I say it with a confidence I don't feel, and I'm sure he can tell. But what should he care so long as he gets laid, right? It doesn't matter if I like him, so long as I don't let down Paul when we finally do it. *Do it.* Hello again, middle school.

He laughs softly and studies my face. "You know what? Never mind. You're not ready. Go swim in the kiddie pool a little longer. I've got better things to do than babysit." Turning away, he puts his hand up in a dismissive wave as he walks off.

What? I finally worked up my nerve, and he turns me down? No freaking way! That's unacceptable. Forgetting that five minutes ago I didn't know him, and two minutes ago I wanted to run away, I charge after him, grab his arm and pull. It's like wrapping my fingers around warm steel.

When he looks at me, his eyes are shrewd and narrow, and that infuriating smirk is still plastered on his face, like he was expecting my reaction. Is he playing me? I don't even know why I want him anymore, other than that he's thrown down the gauntlet and it's now or never. There's no way I'll work up the courage to go through this again.

I glare at Gavin, daring him to contradict me. "I am *so* ready."

He arches a single, skeptical eyebrow, but he nods. "Alright. If you say so. I've got a place around the corner. Don't say I didn't warn you." His smug words taunt me, like he still doesn't believe I'm up for the challenge.

I'm sure he's playing me, but I'll play him right back.

2 ANGIE

The elevator takes forever, and it's really awkward. At least for me. I don't know him, but I'm going to have sex with him, and he's standing there like he doesn't have a care in the world, leaning against the wall with his big, tattooed arms crossed over his chest. Meanwhile, I have to force myself to stand still, my legs wanting to pace the little space we have.

I focus on the yellow lights that slowly tick away our progress towards the thirty-third floor. It's the penthouse, and I'm pretty sure this is the tallest building I've ever been in. Even under the circumstances, I'm amazed at how long the freaking elevators take. I'm probably just a little antsy. Okay, a lot antsy.

Finally, the bell dings and the doors open into a well-lit hallway. It's short, with only three doors, one to either side of us and one straight ahead. Gavin heads for the one on the left, taking the lead. We still haven't said a word since we got in the elevator, but I guess neither of us are here for conversation. It's not like this is a date.

He unlocks it, his heavy key chain rattling. Standing behind him, I admire his broad back, rippling under his tight shirt even at those small movements. I feel small and vulnerable next to him. God, he could break me. *Angie, you've better not have screwed up.*

He gives the door a push and gestures for me to enter with a suave but over the top flourish. Praying that I haven't just done the stupidest thing in my short life, I step forward, drawing a sharp breath as soon as I see the large floor to ceiling windows. Across the room, the whole city sprawls out below us like a quilt made out of neon.

Without thinking about it, I run right up so I can see better. My knees shake with a touch of vertigo, but it's too beautiful to look away. Red and yellow lights glide along the streets far below, like glowing ants scurrying around a giant anthill. Looming over the streets, the buildings are shadowy forms spattered with glowing yellow rectangles showing where someone's home, or working late. I can see the harbor off in the distance, and a large ship's setting out, a floating tower of tiny bright squares. It's amazing. I've never seen a view like this.

Catching my breath, I turn and look around the room with wide eyes while Gavin waits patiently behind me, an expression of amusement on his face. I bet I'm not the first one to come in here and need a moment. Whatever bachelor hovel I'd expected him to have, this isn't it. All of the floors are solid hardwood. Everything is chrome, glass or polished wood, except the large leather couch that faces the biggest TV I've seen in my life. While the windows dominate the whole wall behind me, the others are covered in paintings and artsy photos in fancy frames. Almost every single one features nudes. *That* I might have expected.

Behind the couch, a black marble island separates the living room from a state of the art kitchen that looks like it's hardly been used. No clutter in sight, and there's not a stain or scratch anywhere. I bet if I open the fridge, there won't be anything inside.

The whole place is neat and tidy, like a model apartment that no one lives in.

I don't know who Gavin really is, but he's money and that somehow makes me even more nervous.

There's a large fireplace in the corner that flares up when he hits a switch on the wall, filling the room with silent, flickering light. "I like the real wood ones better." It's the first thing he's said since we left the club. "Gas is convenient, but it's just not the same sound and smell, you know?"

Right, like I'm the type of girl who has opinions on decorative fireplaces that probably cost more than my car. I turn to him. This is all too much. I just need to get it over with. I haven't changed my mind, but it makes me a little sad to think that my first time has turned into something to *get over with*.

When I speak, I hear the tightness in my own voice. "Where's the bedroom?"

He chuckles. "Well, aren't you all business tonight? Fine, this way, babe." Crossing his arms over his torso to peel his t-shirt off as he walks, he casually throws it aside while he leads the way to a closed white door.

I'm glad his back is to me, because while his shirt didn't leave a lot to the imagination, I didn't expect all the ink that covers his massive torso. Abstract designs made with sleek edges and sharp points wrap themselves around his left shoulder and arm. A pair of Chinese dragons in full color spew fire across his back, undulating as he moves. A single lone dove decorates his right side.

Do they mean anything? I want to ask, but it doesn't matter. I'm not here to get to know this guy. He's just taking my cherry. I don't need to know anything about him except that he's good in bed, and something tells me he will be.

As soon as we enter the room, he turns, putting me face to chest with his massive inked pecs. He's chiseled like a Greek god, a masterwork even Michelangelo would've been proud to show off. I get the urge to touch him, to trace the designs on his skin with my finger, but I don't. It feels too personal. *Unlike sex.* This *is* crazy.

Putting his finger underneath my chin, he lifts my gaze to meet his. It's smoldering, his hazel eyes deep and intense. The flecks of color seem to change in the flickering light from the fireplace. Mine feel almost plain in comparison. No matter what he'd said about my eyes earlier at the club, I think I'm the one at risk of getting lost.

He leans close, and I barely get my hands up onto his powerful chest before his lips claim mine. I hadn't meant to kiss him. For some reason it feels more intimate than just *doing it*, but suddenly there's a current running through us, raising all the little hairs on my arms into tingling goosebumps. I don't push him away. Hell, I even kiss him back. God, he feels good.

His hands drop to my shoulders, then slide softly down my back, gliding over the skin exposed by my dress. Experienced fingers find the zipper and tug, sliding it smoothly down towards the small of my back.

Oh crap. It's finally happening. I'm really doing this. Closing my eyes, I try not to think about it too much. I'm doing this for us. For me and Paul.

Right? I couldn't really want this arrogant jerk. He's just a means to an end. My thoughts flit back to Paul and I almost stop right there. Am I doing the right thing? The obvious answer is no, but then I already know that.

I stop thinking. Instead I explore Gavin with my hands, running my fingers across his silky skin, his tight abs, tracing the inky designs that cover him. His body's so hard, so strong. He can do anything he wants to me and there's nothing I can do to stop him. I've put myself right into his power, which is both incredibly scary and ridiculously sexy. There's intense heat building inside me, making want to get out of my suddenly too warm clothes.

He's happy to help, sliding my dress off my shoulders and down my arms before letting it drop to pool around my ankles. I'm standing here in just my underwear and heels, vulnerable and terrified, yet shivering with need. How does his touch do this to me so easily? If I'd felt this with Paul, there's no way I'd have been able to wait. It seems so wrong. I shouldn't be wanting Gavin more than my actual boyfriend.

His hot fingers trace across my skin, sliding over my sides and down to my hips, then cupping my ass and pulling me closer. He's still wearing his pants, but the large bulge is unmistakable as it presses against my stomach. I shiver in fear, or anticipation.

Tracing a path along my jaw and down into the

crook of my neck, his soft lips kiss and nibble their way across my skin. With one hand still holding me close, he glides his other up my back until he reaches the catch on my bra. I draw a sharp breath, holding it.

The lacy garment gives, going slack around me as his clever fingers release it with a practiced ease. My breath comes out in a shudder while he hooks his finger between the cups and tugs. That infuriating smirk still covers his handsome face, but his eyes are dark with desire. I'm not the only one affected.

Heat rushes to my face and down my front as my breasts are exposed. My nipples could cut glass, they're so hard. When his hand starts at my stomach and strokes upwards to cup a breast, I let out a moan. Cassie insisted that first times are supposed to be awkward and terrible, except this is anything but. And if first times can be good, should I even be here?

I find his belt buckle and tug, suddenly eager to move on to the main event. I'm liking this too much, and that's not the point. That can't be the point. Gavin's nothing more than a one night stand to build my confidence, not... whatever this is.

The buckle gives, the fly next. Tugging on his zipper, I work it down until his pants come loose and slide down his thighs. They catch halfway, but he lets go of me long enough to work them down. He never stops kissing my neck, and once his hands are back on me, his lips slide lower, approaching the swell of my breasts.

I'm hyperventilating. I'm going to boil over. His hands are all over me, stroking, squeezing, caressing, making me feel like there are two of him, even three. Expertly, he makes me tingle and shiver under his touch, building my anticipation until I think I'll explode.

Just as he takes a nipple in his mouth, he hooks his fingers in the elastic of my panties, and as he swirls his tongue around the hard point, he tugs, exposing parts of me that no man has ever seen.

The first brush of air against my sex drives home the reality of what I'm doing, and it washes over me like a bucket of ice water. I have a boyfriend. *And I'm cheating on him.* Letting another guy see me naked before Paul ever has. So maybe Paul's never made me feel like this, but that's no excuse. I was crazy for thinking this was a good idea.

"Wait." I take a step back, my nipple slipping out of his mouth with a soft pop, and my panties still halfway down my thighs. "I—I can't do this."

"Hey, it's alright, babe. I'll be gentle." He slides his hands along my sides, his touch slow and seductive. "I'm not going to hurt you."

I swallow, trying to ignore the tingles his talented fingers create along my skin. I repeat myself with more conviction. "No, I mean it. I can't."

He stares at me, his face—and other things—, hard. "Are you fucking kidding me? You're saying this now?"

I rip my eyes away from the huge bulge in his black underwear. "I'm sorry. I really am. I thought I could, but I can't. I'm sorry," I repeat pathetically, yanking my panties back up as fast as I can, and hurriedly picking my bra up off the floor, unable to look him in the eyes. "I shouldn't be here. Damn it."

"Seriously?" He's incredulous, and I don't blame him. I'm angry at myself for thinking I could be okay with this. "Little Miss Let's Get This Over With?" He tugs his underwear down, and my eyes go wide at the sight of his huge dick springing free. He gestures at it with a sneer. "Not even a sympathy blowjob? I'm sure a cocktease like you has had plenty of experience keeping guys out of your pants. You owe me that much."

My cheeks burn, but I catch myself licking my lips. What's wrong with me? I pick up my dress as quickly as I can and run for the door. "I'm sorry. I can't." As I snatch my purse off the leather couch, I feel my chest tighten and wet tears form in the corners of my eyes. I'm such an idiot.

The last thing I hear from Gavin is a frustrated groan, "You've gotta be fucking kidding me!"

I shut the door behind me, finally taking the time to slip my dress back on before hitting the down button on the elevator. I push it over and over like it'll come faster that way, praying he doesn't come out before I'm gone.

Good job, Angie. Good freaking job. I can't even get no-pressure sex right.

My senses are all focused at his door, waiting for it to open, but it doesn't sound like he's following. In fact, I hear the heavy metallic click of a lock. It's an angry, accusative sound that makes my heart ache even though I should be glad he's letting me go with nothing but a few well-earned insults.

The elevator dings, a soft, pleasant chime that's in total contrast to how I'm feeling, then I'm inside, my stomach surging as I start the slow descent back to reality.

I'm never listening to Cassie again.

3 ANGIE

"So." Mom looks at me from across the kitchen table, the corners of her soft eyes crinkled in concern. The delicious smell of dinner cooking in the oven fills the room, though I hardly notice, lost in my own thoughts.

It's been almost three weeks since The Incident, as I've come to think of it, and I've been on edge since, hardly leaving the house. I've hardly spoken to Paul, though he's called a couple of times, wanting me to come over. Mostly to fool around, I think. I just don't know how to face him after what I did, or almost did, depending on how you look at it. One stupid night, and now suddenly everything feels weird and wrong.

I'm sure Mom's noticed, but I haven't brought it up and she's let me be. I doubt that's what she wants to talk about, though. She's never liked Paul anyway. Not even Cassie knows exactly what happened that night, since I haven't been willing to talk to her either. It's stupid to be mad at her, since it's not like she forced me out on my one-night-stand attempt at gunpoint or anything. I still am, though.

I put down my book and meet Mom's gaze with raised eyebrows, trying to forget about my messed up life for a few minutes and inviting her to continue.

"You remember Herbert, right?" She's playing with the hem of her shirt nervously. Usually that means she's going to tell me something I don't like, or that she's nervous. It doesn't happen often though, and I get a funny feeling about this conversation. "The man who's been visiting my flower shop."

Yeah, I remember him. The guy she's been seeing for a few months now, even if she refuses to come out and say it. I think it's kind of cute.

Mom's got a little shop that she's been running for years. It's not doing that great. Everything was good for a couple of years, but then the neighborhood gentrified, rent skyrocketed, and some unexpected maintenance killed her budget. She might have to close, which is really too bad. Me and that shop are her whole world, and I'm about to head off to college.

Herbert is a super-rich CEO type. Apparently he came in one day to buy a bouquet, and somehow they hit it off. It sounds like something out of a cheesy romcom, but she's happy, so I hope it lasts. She's been alone a long time.

Four years, eighty-two days, but who's counting?

I put on an encouraging smile. "Yeah, sure. Well, not that you've let me meet him yet. Why, what's up?" This is it, right? When she finally admits they're a couple? I get why she'd be nervous, but this seems over the top.

She smiles, but it doesn't take away any of the anxiousness. Her fingers have left her dress, but now they're tapping a tattoo on the table, her long nails clacking quickly on the imitation wood. Her anxiety brings it out in me too, and I have to consciously keep my fingers in place so I don't do the same as her. She's about to spring something big.

Straightening in her chair, she chews her lip nervously. "Angie. This is going to seem really sudden." She clears her throat. "You know I loved your father. I still do, but he's been gone four years."

Oh God, she had to go *there*. Even now, my chest gets tight. I was fourteen when it happened, but it hurts just as much now as it did then. Dad was a hot shot helicopter pilot in the Navy, but after flying who knows how many missions in Iraq, he was given the option to come home and become an instructor and he jumped at the chance.

We'd been so happy. He'd finally be home with us and we could be a normal family. Then a few years later, he led what was supposed to be a routine exercise, teaching a couple of students to fly in formation. They were barely off the pads when one of the helicopters veered into his and they both hit the ground.

Nobody survived.

It's ironic. All that time praying for him overseas in combat, and it was some green kid at the academy who ruined it all. We knew there were always risks with flying, but it doesn't mean I miss him any less.

Mom watches me silently, probably knowing what I'm thinking, and waiting for me to give her my attention again. It was hard for both of us. I swallow back the big lump in my throat, then give her a slight nod.

"After I met Herbert… well, I've begun to remember some of the things I missed. Having a partner, someone to confide in, to be close to." She notices my sharp look. "Honey, of course we're a team. You also fill a lot of those roles, but it's not the same. You're about to set out and start your life for real. The thought of my little girl moving out breaks my heart." She smiles fondly. "But I'm also so proud of you. My baby, going to college. Pre-med, no less."

God, this lump's just getting bigger. Dad. Mom gushing. If this is just the lead up to her big revelation, I'm in trouble. Whatever she has on her heart, I don't think it's going to make the lump any smaller.

She puts her hand on my knee. "Herbert will never replace your father, but, he's beginning to fill some of those roles. Faster than I would've thought possible. He's strong, and possessive and caring, and… and I've fallen in love with him." Her eyes are wide and teary, she's so nervous. She knows how much I miss Dad.

It does hurt a bit, but I don't think I've ever seen

her so terrified, so I hurry to smile. It's not like I wasn't expecting it sooner or later. "That's great, Mom. Really." It's true. She does need someone, and I can't be that person. It's not the same. But he's not Dad. "I'm happy for you."

Her relief is obvious, the way her shoulders and face relax, the way she eases back a bit in her chair. She swallows thickly. "That's not everything." Licking her lips, she picks her words carefully. "Herbert proposed to me last night."

My heart stops, and I can almost feel the blood draining from my face. Dating, sure. Overnights, awkward but fine. Proposed? She has to be kidding me. It slowly dawns on me that she wouldn't me telling me this if she'd said no. I look at Mom expectantly, willing her to continue. "And…"

She closes her eyes briefly. "And… I said yes. I'm sorry, hon, I should've spoken to you first. It's just the two of us now, and I shouldn't have—"

"Mom!" She looks up, startled. Sure, I'm freaked out, but if she's found happiness, then it's definitely not my place to get in the way, even if I'm screaming inside. This is going to require some serious thought later, but for now I put on the biggest grin I can and throw my arms around her neck. "I'm so happy for you. Congratulations!"

"Really? You're sure? You have no idea how terrified I've been to tell—"

"Yes!" I cling to her. I am happy. Concerned, but happy. "You deserve it, Mom. But he better not try to make me call him Dad or anything, alright?" I try to sound like I'm joking, but I'm not really.

Apparently I don't hide it well enough. Mom peels me off her and puts me at arm's reach. She looks me in the eyes like she always does when she's being earnest. "Never. You guys will have to find your own relationship and what works for you. I'm just terrified that you'll think I made a huge mistake."

I shake my head softly. "No, Mom. So long as you're happy, I'll be happy. That's the only requirement I have for him. That he makes you happy." I've never been good at strict, but I frown and try to look serious. "And if he doesn't, I'll take him out."

She gives me that look. The one where she's not sure if I'm joking or not. "Well, let's hope it doesn't come to that, alright?" A smile passes between us, and everything's good again. Then the doorbell rings.

"Expecting someone?"

Mom gets up to answer the door. She stops, smooths down her skirt and checks herself in the mirror. She usually wears a little makeup, but I suddenly realize it's more than usual. And how did I miss those bright red lips?

"I asked him over for dinner. I thought it'd be a good chance for you guys to get to know each other better." She pauses for a minute. "Oh, he has a son. I should've mentioned that. He's a bit rough around the edges from what I've seen, but Herbie insists that he's a good guy underneath it all. So you'll have a stepbrother now, too." She throws me a brief smile, then hurries to the front door.

Herbie? And a stepbrother? She definitely could've mentioned that earlier. Not that it changes how I feel about anything, but I like to have all the facts so I can prepare. I got that from Dad, I think. Him and his checklists. I stand, take a deep breath and smooth down my shirt. Alright, let's get this over with. A brother might not be bad. I'd always wanted a sibling. Better late than never I guess.

Their voices carry through the house from the entry. Herbert's voice is deep and gravelly, like he used to smoke. Or still does, I suppose, but that doesn't sound like Mom's type. I give them a moment to say their hellos before I approach.

"Hello… um…" I just realize I have no idea what to call him.

He smiles warmly, his face looking strangely familiar. Square jaw, deep hazel eyes. He holds out his hand. "Herbert's fine. You must be Angela."

I take it. "Just Angie. Thanks."

"You give your girl a nice name, but will she use it?"

Mom's always disliked me shortening my name, but Angela makes me feel like I'm eighty. Maybe because she named me after her great aunt Angela who used to make me watch Jeopardy marathons. Given her use of *Herbie* earlier, it really feels like a double standard.

Herbert takes a step to the side. "I'd like you to meet my son, Gavin, the heir apparent to my financial empire. A bit of a rebellious streak, but I'm working on it." He smirks in a scarily familiar way.

My jaw drops. No way. No fucking way. The floor drops out from under me at the mention of his name. This isn't happening. No wonder his facial structure looks so familiar. Like father, like son.

Like my new stepbrother, who I almost fucked just three weeks ago. He puts his hand out like his dad did, his gorgeous eyes locked to mine. He's grinning broadly, obviously thinking this is the funniest thing in the world. "Hi there, Sis."

I stand still so long that Mom gives me a bump with her elbow. Her whisper is a hiss, though I'm sure they all hear it. "Angela."

Like a rusty robot, I raise my arm stiffly and take his, remembering the rough feel of his large hands all over me as I shake it briefly. Even that short touch sends sparks racing up the skin of my arms. I should say something, but I've no idea what.

"Hi." That's all I get out, then I just stand there like an idiot.

Mom gives me a confused we'll-talk-about-this-later look, but she shoves me aside and makes room for our visitors. "Come in, come in. I've got a roast cooking in the oven and potato gratin and asparagus to go with it. It should be done in twenty minutes or so." She practically drags Herbert towards the living room, leaving me alone with Gavin.

4 ANGIE

"Well, how's this for a surprise?" Gavin laughs out loud, a rumble in his powerful chest. "And here I thought you were gone from my life for good."

I finally find my words, hissing them between my teeth. "Fine, laugh it up. But not a word about this to anyone. You eat, we stay pleasant, and then you leave. You understand?"

"I don't know, babe. I'm not nearly as good at leaving as you are. Will you teach me how? Besides, this is like destiny. Karma. It's like God decided to give me a second chance." His voice drips with sarcasm. He strikes his arms out, smiling broadly. "Beautiful Angie, delivered right into my arms." Closing in until his nose is only an inch from mine, he whispers loudly. "What do you think? Should we do it in your bed? That'd be hot."

The image of the two of us in my bed, him naked and above me flashes through my mind. I must've given something away, because his smile broadens knowingly. He's so frustrating. I want to smack him right in the face, but I hold back. This isn't the time to make a scene. Also, he doesn't seem to care if anyone finds out that he almost boned his stepsister, but I do, and I don't want him to have any excuse to blab.

Instead, I try to reason. "Gavin. If anyone finds out that we almost... well, you know, then—"

"Almost what? I think you need to explain it more clearly." He laughs, enjoying my misery. "Did we almost do something three weeks ago? My memory's a bit fuzzy. I think you have to be more specific."

So much for reasoning. "You're a prick, Gavin." Turning on my heels, I stomp out of the entry, leaving him laughing behind me. Why did it have to be him? And why is my heart pounding like a jackhammer?

* * * * *

I'm so nervous I can barely eat, but Gavin's a totally different person at dinner. He's well spoken, respectful, polite, friendly… and only I seem to realize that it's all a sham. With a long sleeved and collared shirt on, his ink isn't visible anywhere. The hair that was so wild three weeks ago is combed neatly and gelled into place. I want to scream that this isn't really who he is, but who's going to believe me? And what would that do, other than ruin dinner?

I sigh. This is supposed to be Mom's night, where she gets to bask in being newly engaged. I shouldn't be messing it up. If he can pretend, then I can too. Swallowing my dislike, I close my eyes for a moment before I engage in the conversation. Mom smiles in relief, her shoulders relaxing. This isn't going to be easy.

We're about halfway through our meal when I feel his foot sliding up my shin. Our eyes meet, his mischievous sparkle crashing into my ice cold disdain. What the hell does he think he's doing? I try to push him away with my other foot, but there's only so much I can do without being really obvious. In the end, I settle for an angry glare while I do my best to ignore him. Or rather, bide my time.

Mom's just refilled the wine glasses, even half a glass for me, which makes Gavin grin crookedly. When I reach for the salt, an idea strikes. In an accident that's totally on purpose, I knock over his glass, right towards his lap. Wine splashes everywhere, but mostly onto his shirt and pants. I can't believe I just did that, but when I see his shocked expression, I feel no regret whatsoever.

"Oops!" It's the most halfhearted *oops* in the history of *oopses*.

He glares at me, grabbing his napkin and dabbing at his clothes. They look expensive, but whatever. He can afford it. Maybe next time he'll reconsider playing footsie with someone who isn't interested. He looks up, and since Mom and Herbert are scrambling to help wipe up, I stick my tongue out.

His expression darkens, his eyebrows furrowing and his lips tightening in an angry scowl. Is he going to blow already? I didn't think he'd be that easy. His eyes grow stormy, and I watch him, holding my breath, just waiting for the explosion. He surprises me. The storm blows over almost immediately, and instead of frowning, his face relaxes before spreading back into a friendly smile. While Mom fusses over him and Herbert dabs a napkin at the wine on the floor, Gavin mouths two words at me, "Well played."

Oh, the game is on, rich boy.

"I'm so sorry, Gavin." Mom's found a cloth that she's brushing against his shirt.

"It's alright. That's what dry-cleaners are for. Some people are just naturally clumsy." He pulls the cloth from her hands. "Honestly, don't worry about it. But maybe there's a restroom I could borrow for a moment."

Mom's still frowning and throws me a we'll-talk-about-this-later-too expression, but she nods. "Of course. Why don't you use the one upstairs? It's bigger. I'm sure *Angela* can show you where it is." I don't miss the stress she puts on my name, a warning if I ever heard one.

"Of course, Mom." I keep my tone even in my best good little girl voice, but the last thing I want is to be alone with him. Still, what's he going to do with our parents right below us? "This way." He follows me closely. "I'll try not to trip and push you down the stairs," I whisper. "But I'm so *naturally clumsy*. Maybe you should go first."

"Oh no. Please. Show the way."

Rolling my eyes, I climb the stairs. We're barely halfway up when his heavy hands land on my hips to stop me, much as I was afraid of. They're strong and even through my jeans they feel hot. He's standing one step below, but he's tall enough he has to lean down to whisper into my ear, "If you want my pants off so badly, you only had to ask, Sis." His chuckle raises the hairs at the back of my neck, and his husky whisper fills me with heat. Damnit, I don't want to be attracted to him.

"Don't call me sis. I'm not your sis. I'll never be your sis." Each phrase comes out a little icier than the one before it. "Now let me go."

He holds his hands up in the air. "Of course. Anything you say, *Sis*."

I want to scream, but that would only bring Mom here running. Instead I clench my hands into tight fists. My nails dig into my palms, but the pain gives me something to focus on. Instead of the big, stupid, annoying, bratty, incredibly handsome guy behind me.

I get to the top, open the door to the right for him and gesture inside. "The master bath. Would there be anything else?" I tell him acidly.

"Well… there is one thing—"

"Don't even try it. Do you really want me anywhere near your vulnerable body parts right now? *Really?* What if I slip and bite it off?"

"I was just going to ask which towel I should use, but thanks for the warning." He backs into the bathroom, grinning as I let out a growl. "Thanks, Sis." With a laugh, he shuts the door.

Arrgh! I stomp back downstairs, then pause to give myself a minute to relax my features. With my happy daughter mask back on, I return to the dinner table. Mom throws me a thankful glance, but I'm sure I'll hear about the wine glass later. Gavin returns after a couple of minutes, looking drier, but still with big burgundy stains on his shirt and pants. He winks at me and sits as if nothing ever happened.

When dinner's over, I offer to clear the table, just to keep out of the way. Of course that ass does the same. It makes Mom smile. "That's very nice of you kids. I'll take this wonderful wine Herbert brought and we'll have glasses ready for you in the living room when you're done. I've even got some of that sparkling grape juice you like, Angela." Then she and my future stepdad glide out of the dining room, arm in arm. And here I thought being eighteen meant being an adult.

Gavin looks at me. "So…" He draws it out. "How about your mom's bed? If we're quick, she'll never know." He pats me on the ass.

Oh, for—

I'm only one poor decision away from picking up the sauce boat and flinging it at his head. "Not in my room, not in Mom's bed, not ever. Got it?" I stick my tongue out at him again. "Prick."

"Oh real mature there, *Sis*." He rubs it in, putting pressure on the word to make sure I hear him.

I whirl on him, almost dropping the sauce boat and potatoes in the process. "I already told you, don't you dare call me that. I'm not your fucking sis, and you're not my freaking *bro*." I'm done. There was a breaking point, and I hit it. "I'd rather you didn't talk to me at all, to be honest." With a snarl, I put him behind me and stride into the kitchen.

He shows up a moment or two later, balancing a

scarily tall stack of plates, silverware and a couple of glasses. I rush over to grab the top ones. "Jesus, you don't have to carry all of them at once. What if they'd fallen?"

"I would've paid for new ones?" He shrugs after putting the stuff down on the kitchen table.

Of course. Throw money at it. "Believe it or not, it's not that easy. They haven't made that set in ages. I wouldn't have to kill you. Mom would."

"Alright, alright. Fuck. How was I supposed to know they were family heirlooms?"

They aren't. They're the set Mom and Dad bought when they were first married, but I'm not about to tell him that. I start putting stuff in the sink, figuring Mom and Herbert want some time alone. I can always wash some of the pieces that don't go in the dishwasher. Anything to keep busy.

"Thanks, you can leave now."

I sense Gavin moving just a split second before his hands come down on either side of me and grip the edge of the sink. He moves close, until his front's pressing against my back.

"I could do you over the sink. They're snuggled up in the living room. They'll never know." His breath is hot against my ear, and his bulge presses into the small of my back.

"Are you deaf? What part of 'I don't want anything to do with you' and *leave* didn't you understand?" I whirl around, but it only presses my breasts into him instead, and that doesn't help. It's hard to think when he's so close. He didn't button his shirt all the way up after trying to clean off the wine stains, and I can see a bit of ink peeking out. The image of his naked chest is burned into my brain even though I wish I could scrub it out.

"I heard your words." He leans in like he's going to kiss me. My breath speeds up and my heart starts pounding. Even if my mind thinks he's despicable, my body knows differently. He stops short of my mouth. "I just don't think you meant them. Admit you want me. Just a little?" His teasing voice both excites and infuriates me.

I'm just about to say something when his hand comes to my hip, sliding slowly up along my waist, the heat of him almost unbearable. For a second I close my eyes, distracted by his touch, before I force them back open. I check the doorway, expecting Mom and my stepfather-to-be staring at us in shock.

There's no one there, but even just the thought gets me moving. I dodge to the side to get away from his touch, clutching the kitchen counter behind me. "Leave me alone. I should never have gone with you in the first place, and it sure as hell didn't become any more appropriate now."

"Fine, suit yourself." He shrugs, opens the cabinet under the sink and finds the garbage can. Beginning to clear the plates into it, he glances up at me. "I'll rinse, and you can load the dishwasher."

I blink, caught off guard by his change of gears. He's already rinsing and looks at me, daring me to make a scene about nothing. When I come closer, it's cautiously, like a skittish animal approaching a wolf. "Alright." I open the dishwasher without taking my eyes off him. "But no funny stuff. I mean it."

"Of course." He smirks, making me want to wipe it right off him. "Here." He hands me the first rinsed plate. I keep waiting for the other shoe to drop, but it's not long before we're done, and I'm almost convinced we're past it. I close the dishwasher and turn towards the living room.

I'm just about there, when he whips a towel and catches me right on the ass. "Good work, Sis."

Of course he gets me just as I'm entering the living room, so all I can do is hiss out of the corner of my mouth, "I'm not your sis." He laughs and pats me on the shoulder like we're buddies and I just said something funny.

"Oh, there you guys are." Mom and Herbert turn towards us. "We were wondering if we were going to have to come in and get you." Mom's smiling, like she's happy to see us getting along. I can't screw this up for her.

I shrug. "Oh, you know, we're just talking."

Mom's gentle smile turns into a mischievous grin. "Better not be any hanky panky. You're going to be siblings, you know."

They laugh it up while I just want to crawl into a hole and hide. My face is blushing so hot it must be glowing. This is one of the worst days ever. Second only to The Incident. What do those two things have in common? Oh right, *Gavin.*

The devil speaks up. "I wouldn't think of it, ma'am. I'll be on my best behavior." His arrogant smirk smooths right into a sweet smile that's like he specially designed it to melt the hearts of girlfriends' mothers. Maybe he did. He probably practices it in front of the mirror every morning.

"Oh, Gavin. Call me Marie." Of course the smile's working.

"Of course, Marie. Thank you."

Aaarrgh!

Herbert clears his throat. "I'd like your attention for a moment." He smoothly pulls two envelopes out of the inner pocket of his blazer. "As you all know, I asked for Marie's hand in marriage yesterday, and I think it's a cause for celebration."

I hold my breath. This sounds big.

"Marie, I've gotten us tickets on the Golden Emperor of the Seas, the most exclusive cruise ship in the world. Two weeks in the utmost of luxury. What do you say? A little celebration, and maybe a surprise or two."

Holy crap, that sounds expensive. I glance at Gavin, finding his face surprisingly hard, his narrowed eyes glaring at Mom. What's that all about?

"Herbie." Mom's eyes are glistening, filling up with tears. "I—I wish you'd asked me first."

"Why? What's wrong?" Herbert's eyes narrow, and I see the family resemblance.

"I—Oh, God, this is embarrassing—I get

seasick. Violently. I can barely look at a boat without throwing up. The idea of spending a couple of weeks on one terrifies me." She watches Herbert's face closely as it stiffens. "I'm—I'm sorry."

He blinks, and then slowly, his lips curl upwards. He breaks into loud laughter, throwing the tickets onto the table. "Go figure." He smiles at her, and for a moment I'm jealous of my own mother, because I want someone to look at me like that. "Nothing to be sorry about, darling. We'll just find something else. You're right. I should've asked first." He looks a bit embarrassed.

"Well, I didn't make dessert, but I did buy some cookies. Let me go get them." Mom gets up, straightening her skirt.

Herbert is up just as quickly. "I'll join you, and get rid of these." His eyes sparkle with mischief as he picks up the cruise tickets. They head to the kitchen together, Mom walking with a wiggle I don't think I've seen her use in my whole life. With Herbert walking behind her, I suppose I know why, though. He casually drops the tickets into the recycling bin as he passes by.

He's going to throw them out? Just like that?

Must be nice to be a freaking billionaire. I take a moment to imagine myself on a cruise ship, soaking up sun, drinking sangrias. And not sparkling grape juice. "I think I'll get some water."

Gavin grabs my wrist. "I wouldn't, unless you want to catch your mom making out."

I blink, a number of terrifying images flashing before my eyes. Making out? Oh God. I sit back down, glancing over at him to see if he's serious. He shrugs. Alright, I suppose I can wait.

"Gotta piss." Gavin gets up.

Yuck! "Thanks for sharing." Some guys can't do anything without narrating it.

"There's a bathroom downstairs, right? Where is it, Sis?"

I sigh deeply, making sure he realizes just annoying he is. "Down the hall, second door on the left. And I'm not your sis."

"Thanks, Sis."

Arrrgh!

Laughing and flirting, Mom and Herbert return with the cookies. They sit down together on the love seat, and talk like I'm not even there. Who'd ever thought Mom would make me feel like the third wheel? Oh, whatever. At least the kitchen should be safe now. They don't even notice me leave.

I pour a glass of what's left of the wine from dinner, then turn and lean against the counter while drinking it. Today's been ridiculous. I need to get away a while, at least if Gavin's going to be hanging around. I *so* can't deal with him on a regular basis.

That's when I spot them, lying on top of the recycling. Two crisp, shiny tickets, about to go to waste. Snagging them quickly, I examine closer. The ship leaves tomorrow night and comes back about two weeks later. All inclusive. Exclusive cruise. A top floor suite. My mind starts to whirr.

Herbert's already forgotten about the tickets, of course. I knew he was money, but I still can't believe how he'll just throw away something that most people would think of as the vacation of a lifetime. We're not exactly poor, but we've always had to save for everything. Meanwhile, he's on another planet where money doesn't matter.

I guess if they get married, we'll be like that too, but it feels like cheating, somehow. Not that I'm going to med school for the money, but I always considered a high income one of the perks. Well, I'm not going to mooch off him either way. I'll make my own freaking money. I've got my self-respect.

What I don't have though, is a summer job. There's nothing tying me down, and Paul's not working either. Wonder what he'd say to a fancy cruise. Since the whole Gavin thing, I've been kind of avoiding him and I can tell it's pissing him off. Having our first time onboard a luxury cruise has got to be make up for something, right?

So maybe I'll mooch just a little.

Palming the tickets, I get up and rush to my room to call him, already digging my cell out of my pocket. We're going on a cruise!

5 GAVIN

Fuck, I've had to piss since I got here. I knew I forgot something when I was getting the wine stains out. This politeness shit grates on my nerves, but while Dad tolerates me—under doubt—most of the time, he'd cut me off completely if I did anything to fuck up family night with his fiancée. I don't know what he's expecting me to do, but he's been so damn uptight about tonight that I'm tempted to go out there and be the asshole he apparently thinks I am.

I take my time, in no rush to get back to the lovebirds. Or Angie. Fucking Angie. Like I needed another reason to think about her, when it's all I've been doing for the past three weeks. Why? No idea.

Maybe because she's the first girl to turn me

down, leaving me blue-balled and alone. Usually I'm the one that's doing the running, but she left me high and dry. Didn't even look back. She's drop-dead fucking gorgeous, of course, but so are most of the girls I fuck. Or fucked. After that night, my heart hasn't been in it. Three weeks is the longest I've gone in years. What's so fucking magical about her pussy?

Other than the fact that I haven't been in it.

Is it really that simple? I just want what I can't have? That would be nice, because I know the cure, and it's between her legs. But the whole stepsister thing? That was a surprise and a fucking half. I'm supposed to stop noticing how hot she is just because our parents are screwing? No way. Just gets me harder. There's something seriously hot about the idea of bending my brand new stepsister over her bed and fucking her silly. Hell, if our parents are downstairs, that's just bonus.

Alright, gotta think of something else, or I'll be fucking standing here all night, waiting for my hardon to ease up. There's always my hand, I guess, but after three weeks, my hand and me are really getting to know each other way too well. At least we're thinking about the same girl.

It's tempting, but no way. I'm not going to jerk off in their ratty old bathroom like a loser. Maybe I'll go out after this and get laid. Find someone, fuck them and move the hell on.

I tuck myself in, zip up, wash up, and head back to the living room.

Where no one is. Great. I don't even want to know what Dad and my newest in a long line of stepmoms are up to in the kitchen. Let her dig for her gold. Angie was the only entertaining thing here. Where'd she go? Sitting around alone sounds boring as fuck.

I hear her voice, faintly. Following it, I head up their carpeted stairs. Maybe she's in her room. Right away, my thoughts fill with all the dirty, filthy things I'd like to do to her there. I'm imagining it all little girl still, with pink wallpaper and horse pictures on the walls. My pants feel tighter as I react to the thought of her on her hands and knees on her bed, her perfect naked ass facing me. Jesus, this girl's gonna kill me and she doesn't even realize it. I really need to get laid.

At the top of the stairs, I pause, listening to her sexy voice coming clearly through a partially open door. She's on the phone, it sounds like. I probably shouldn't be listening, but she sounds excited and I'm curious. Is she talking about me?

"No, I'm serious, Paul. A cruise, a real live luxury cruise. All paid for. I've already got the tickets. Just pack and meet me down at the pier tomorrow at eight. Yeah, PM. Everything's covered." Her voice is excited, but who's she talking to? Paul? Friend? Boyfriend? Also, it's hilarious that she grabbed the tickets. It's difficult not to laugh out loud. She's got more balls than I've given her credit for. Love it.

"Alright. Awesome." Something comes into her voice, like a really sexy promise. "You totally don't want to miss out on this trip. I think I'm ready." She waits, listening. "Yeah, that's exactly what I mean, and you don't want to miss out on that, do you? I promise I'll make up for how I've been acting the past couple weeks."

I probably wouldn't have a clue what she was talking about if we hadn't had that episode at the club. I have a really good idea what's caused her trouble with *Paul* and it's good to know I'm not the only one hung up on that night. Fuck that noise. I gotta find out who this Paul guy is and put him off this shit. Forget finding some random girl to fuck Angie out of my system. Now it's a competition, and I don't lose.

I get distracted, and suddenly I'm face to face with her as she comes out her door. Shit. "Hey."

Her tone is colder than a goddamn snowman. "What the hell are you doing up here?" She glances down the stairs, probably to make sure no one else hears. "I'm not going to fuck you, Gavin. Not now, not ever."

"What? You're probably a shitty lay anyway. I'd just be doing you a favor." I don't even mean to insult her, but she gets this look and crap comes out my mouth before I can stop it. Pisses me off too, because suave is what I do best.

Fucking hell, I never imagined she could look that angry. She blanches and her eyes turn into slits. I'm half expecting to see smoke coming out of those cute little ears. She lifts her finger and pushes it right into my chest. "You're a fucking asshole." It sounds so sexy when she says it. "I'm going to do my best to tolerate you, since it sounds like our parents are getting hitched, but I swear, if you don't stop following me around, I'll get a freaking restraining order, regardless of what our parents think. Clear?"

I back off. We both know she wants me, but I'm not stupid enough to push again tonight. "Clear as crystal. I'm sorry."

"What?" She actually looks confused for a second.

"I said I'm sorry. I was out of line." See? I can do polite.

Confusion turns to suspicion. "Since when do *you* apologize?"

"It happens. Don't get too used to it." Why does everyone assume the worst of me?

She sighs. "Alright. Fine. Thanks. Can we go back downstairs now?"

"Sure." I let her go first, if only so I can watch her ass swing on the way down. "So who's Paul?"

She stops, but doesn't turn. "Seriously? You're listening in on my phone calls?"

"I can't help it if you're a screamer. Sorry. Didn't know you were on the super-secret red phone to the president." Okay, so maybe I'm a bit of an asshole. But she loves me, she just doesn't know it yet.

She starts to walk again. "For your information, he's my boyfriend."

For now. "Yeah?"

"Yeah. So there's another reason for you to keep your hands off me." There's acid dripping from that voice.

"So... where was Paul when my hands *were* all over you?"

"I told you that was a mistake."

"Alright, alright." Sighing, I back off. "So what's this guy like? Big and buff? Sweeps you off your feet? Makes you feel like a princess?"

She laughs. "What? Jealous? Yeah, he's good looking. He wants me for me. Not just because I, in a serious lapse of judgement, threw myself into his arms at some scuzzy club."

"Sounds lame." We're back in the living room, but still no sign of our parents. I don't even want to know. "How'd you meet him?"

Angie's pale skin flushes. "Actually, it *was* at a scuzzy club." She gives me a pointed don't-you-dare-judge look. "But he stuck out from the crowd. Tall, sexy. Gorgeous green eyes. He's got a scar down his face, but it only adds to the look, you know. Makes him seem a little dangerous."

Scar down his face? Paul? Shit. "Paul Cartman?"

Her jaw drops as she stares at me in surprise. "Are you following me around or something? *Should* I be getting a restraining order?"

"Jesus, no. It's just that I know him. Well, know of him. That's all." I know of him alright. Like how he's got his nose full of fucking cocaine more often than not. And that he's got at least one more girl. Violet, I think her name is. He's fucking scum, and Angie's too fucking good for him. That makes this easy. I won't even feel bad when I fuck her right out from under his powdery nose.

My face must have shown something of what I was thinking, since she looks at me curiously. "Why? Something I should know about him?"

"What? Nah, nothing. Don't worry about it." My hands are already clenching and unclenching. I'd better get out of here. "Listen, I need to jet. If our parents ever surface, could you tell them I had to go?" I shrug. "Just realized I had somewhere to be."

She looks at me with suspicion, but seems just as happy to see me leave. "Yeah, okay."

I feel kind of successful. That's about the most civil bit of conversation we've had so far. "Don't get too sentimental, now. I'll be back to feel you up in no time." Or not.

"I can't wait." Her voice could freeze over the Sahara.

"Of course you can't. I'm irresistible like that." I get the hell out of there before she can respond. I've got a face to pound.

6 ANGIE

It's almost eight thirty. Where the hell's Paul? We should be boarding now. I look over at the ticket guy apologetically. Not that he seems to care. I guess it doesn't matter to him whether we make it onto the boat or not.

An angry roar echoes off the warehouses along the water. Wait, is that him? A motorcycle pulls up, screeching into the parking lot like it's in a car chase. The rider's tall, broad and definitely not Paul. He looks like someone else I know, though. I wait impatiently while he locks the bike and pulls his helmet off.

Yep, it's who I think it is. My step-albatross.

"Hi." Gavin's wearing his trademark smirk.

"What the hell are you doing here?"

"Paul couldn't make it. So I offered to take his place." He looks way too satisfied with himself. That can't be good.

"What did you do?" I step closer, ready to… to do what, exactly? Chew him out, I guess, but somehow I doubt he'll care.

"Me? Nothing. We just discussed, is all. He realized he had other commitments, and I realized that you wouldn't be able to get on your cruise without me." He hefts his suitcase. "So here I am. Ready to do anything to help out family."

Alright, now I know something's up. "What do you mean, not able to leave without you?"

"How closely did you look at the tickets?" The corners of his eyes crinkle with amusement.

"Closely? Depends. What do you mean?" I pull them out of my pocket and look over them. They look identical except different serial numbers. Top deck suite, everything covered, have to be at the dock by 8:45 PM, both tickets in the name of Herbert Caldwell.

Gavin waits while I read, but eventually he runs out of patience. "Red text, just under Dad's name."

The red text is in thin print and hard to make out. Whoever thought red as a text color on a dark blue background made sense was an idiot. I peer closely with an impatient sigh.

ID required.

Crap.

I look up at Gavin, wrinkling my nose at the know-it-all look on his face. "So how are you supposed to save the day? Newsflash, you're not your dad."

"No, that's true." He gets his wallet out of his jeans, tugs out a card and hands it to me. It's his driver's license. *Gavin Herbert Caldwell.* "But I share his name."

I giggle. "Herbert? You?" Sometimes you learn something new about someone that totally alters your idea of who they are. I have no idea why his middle name should be something like that, but for some reason Herbert doesn't match at all in my head with who Gavin is. My giggles turn to laughter. World view: rocked.

"Yeah, yeah, very funny. Give me my license back." There's a tone of childish annoyance in his voice that only gets me laughing harder. I bet he was one of those kids who never admitted his middle name in school. I've suddenly found a vulnerable spot, a chink in his armor, and that's really satisfying. He reaches out and pulls the piece of plastic from between my fingers. "It's a fucking middle name. Get over it."

"Yeah, sure… Herbert." I break down again, my gut hurting. I don't even get why it's so funny anymore, but now I've got a serious case of the giggles.

"You know what? Maybe I'll just go alone." With another quick grab, he nabs the tickets right out of my hand and picks up his suitcase. "More room for me in the bed anyway."

I look up quickly. "Hey, wait. You're not leaving me here now." I've barely left town before, much less gone on a luxury cruise. There's no way I'm letting this opportunity pass me by, even if I have to do it with my asshole stepbrother instead of my boyfriend. I'll totally make it up to Paul when I get back, I swear. Grabbing my suitcase, I rush up the ramp to the ship. "Wait for me!" Gavin doesn't even turn, but he's not walking particularly quickly either. I catch up easily.

"Oh, you decided to come. Going to behave?"

He talks over his shoulder, not even turning to look at me.

"I won't make fun of your name anymore." That's about as much as I can promise. I'm not letting him walk all over me.

"Not what I asked, but whatever. I'll take it." A few words and a flash of his license later, and we're onboard. The hum of the engines warming up dominates everything, making the deck vibrate beneath my feet.

I gawk. This is my first time on something bigger than a small sailboat. I can hardly tell I'm on a ship at all, and not just in a particularly rumbly hotel. A fancy rumbly hotel. Everything's a mixture of polished wood, white and gold, sleek trim and minimal lines. A dash of deep red here and there.

We're standing in a reception area where stewards in fancy white uniforms wait for something to do, their eyes scanning the passengers like a little flock of hyenas. Probably deciding who's likely to give the biggest tips. A line of guests in much fancier dress than me stand ahead of us, getting checked in as quickly as the frazzled desk clerk can process them.

I glance at Gavin, who's looking everywhere but

me. Dressed casually too, he makes me feel less like the odd girl out. Worn jeans, though I'm sure they're designer something or other. A plain black t-shirt, his biker jacket thrown over his shoulder and leather motorcycle boots on his feet. We get a few looks, but whatever. What are they going to do? Throw us off the ship?

He turns to me and catches me watching him. With a grin, he puts his arm around my waist and pulls me close, making me squeak. "Oh Marie," he says, using Mom's name. "I can't wait until we get hitched." He leans in to give me a kiss, but I dodge it. "Oh, come on, babe."

I sigh dramatically. "Not until we're married, Herbie." At first he frowns at the nickname, but it quickly turns to a laugh. He's enjoying this game way too much. And so am I. For now, we're in on this together, and it kind of fun.

He whispers to me loudly, but I don't think anyone else can hear, "I'll have to settle for dreaming of you on our wedding night. On all fours, with your gown up around your waist." He leans closer. "Just waiting for me."

"Well, keep dreaming, since that's as close as

you'll ever get."

He laughs again. "We'll see about that."

I'm about to throw another retort his way when a voice speaks up. "I tell you Mabel, liners these days wouldn't know luxury if it bit them in the ass. Making us stand in line, of all things. Remember back when we were young? When the only pause before a steward showed us to our suite was to pick up a cocktail?" The voice is worn with age, but clear and loud. Also it's right behind us. I peek over my shoulder.

The woman who spoke looks old enough to be my great-grandmother, but she stands tall and her eyes are sharp, scanning the reception critically. Stylish and slim, she carries herself like she's half her age, though that's still old enough to be my mom. Her mouth is a slim straight line as she examines the line in frustration.

"Do you think the—the buffet is open, Joyce?" Standing next to her, hunched over a walker is her companion, who I assume is Mabel from Joyce's tirade. Contrary to her friend, Mabel looks her age, crooked and bent, clutching her handles with shaking hands. Her floral dress, while probably expensive, hangs loosely.

Joyce huffs noisily. "I'm sure it will be soon. Though if the line doesn't start moving faster, I do believe we may meet our end here, Mabel. It's all over." Her tone moves smoothly from frustrated to melodramatic. I'd say she was bitchy, but then I see the way her eyes soften when she looks at her friend, and how she's supporting her while they wait. She's just impatient, and this waiting isn't easy for Mabel.

Well, Mom always said to do the right thing. "Excuse me." I get Joyce's attention, her gaze hawk like again. "I'm sorry. I know it isn't much, but you can go ahead of us at least."

Joyce's expression softens again, and she actually cracks a smile. "Thank you, dearie. It's nice to see that good manners haven't completely died out. Some days…" She trails off while I get out of the way. I'm glad to see Gavin moving as well, but then he frowns a moment. He throws me a sly glance, as if to say *watch this.*

"You know what, ladies? Making you wait like this is unacceptable. Follow me." And as simply as that, he forces his way through the crowd. "Come on, people. Let the ladies through. What kind of misanthropes are you?"

Misanthropes? I'm surprised he even knows the word. Still, the crowd parts reluctantly, letting the four of us past, until we're standing at the desk with the surly concierge glaring up at us. "What's going on?" The couple he was helping, the man in skinny jeans and a polo jacket, the woman in a designer dress and some awfully big and gaudy jewelry, glare at us, their eyes shooting daggers. They obviously want to object, but Gavin's a pretty scary guy when he wants to be. They stay to the side and fume quietly.

He flexes as he leans on the concierge's desk, looking down with pure disdain. His tattoos shift enticingly, though I'm pretty sure that's not what the man in front of him thinks. Gavin's voice is even, calm and full of steel. "I'm not sure what you think customer service is around here, but this sure as hell isn't it."

The concierge sighs dramatically, then explains in a bored voice, as if he's already had to do this several times today, "Sir, we're processing the line as quickly as we can. If you'd just go back to your position—"

"Listen…" Gavin takes a look at his name tag. "Richard. Dick? Can I call you Dick?"

"I—" The concierge doesn't get far.

"Listen, *Dick*, these two ladies have lived far too long to have to wait for a weasel like you. If you guys don't have an express lane for seniors, well, then I'm opening one now. Starting with them." He looms closer for emphasis.

"Sir, we don't— I can't—" Dick is so shocked he can't make words.

"You can and you will." He gestures magnanimously for Joyce and Mabel to step up to the counter, then hangs back just far enough to never leave Dick's field of vision. Crossing his arms over his powerful chest, he glares until the sour concierge helps them check in.

Wow. I don't even know if he's an ass, a hero, or both. I'm glad the two old ladies don't have to wait any longer, but holy crap. *He* obviously doesn't care, but I can feel the eyes of everyone around us boring angrily into my back.

Joyce turns to us with a remarkably childish grin. "Thank you so much, young man. You're a brute, but you used it to our advantage, so we appreciate it."

Gavin shrugs. "I do what I must."

"You do indeed. You remind me a lot of my

fourth husband, actually—" Mabel interrupts her by pulling on her sleeve. "I suppose I'm needed. Thank you again."

I give them a little wave and a smile as they walk towards the elevators. Meanwhile, Gavin's turned back to the counter.

The concierge tries to take charge again. "Sir, you're not a senior. Please get back in—"

"Oh shut up. You want to get rid of us, so here's your chance. Herbert Caldwell and Marie Wilson. We have a suite." Gavin talks right over him, but when he hears the names, it's like the concierge is a whole new person. He lights up, smiling broadly, eager to help. I roll my eyes. What a suck up.

Gavin receives our key cards and hands one to me which I jam in my pocket. He thanks the concierge for his help, then picks up both of our suitcases and sets off towards the elevators with long strides, giving me nothing to do except follow. I catch up, just in time to hear him mumble something like, "…ass-kissing motherfucker."

Maybe not in those words, but for once we agree on something.

KIM LINWOOD

7 ANGIE

The door opens to our room, and even Gavin whistles. "Nice choice, Dad. It's the fucking bridal suite." He steps inside with our suitcases, leaving me in the doorway with my mouth hanging open and my eyes flitting around the room.

Our cabin's huge. Two rooms. The bright white walls are covered with floral murals that are so detailed that I half expect to be able to smell them. I can't keep from running my fingers over everything, like I have to check if it's real.

The room has all the typical hotel room things, a sitting area, a minibar, closets and drawers, but everything looks money. Stainless steel and polished wood. Gold trim. The two love seats are so white I'm afraid to sit down and get them dirty. The pink heart shaped pillows are a little hokey, though.

A gorgeous bouquet of roses stands in a vase on the low glass coffee table, as well as a bucket of champagne and a box of fancy chocolates. I don't know champagne, but I bet it's the good stuff. While Gavin carries our suitcases into the bedroom, I sneak one of the chocolates, and it's amazing. Smooth and delicious, filled with some sort of alcohol that melts in my mouth and warms my stomach.

Large windows line the opposite wall, framing a door that leads out to a huge balcony. It opens easily, and crisp ocean air fills my lungs as I step out into the night. This close to the city, there aren't a lot of stars out, but the view from this high up is breathtaking. Not quite as nice as Gavin's apartment, but close.

I should check out the bedroom, if only to make sure Gavin isn't rooting through my underwear or something. I peek my head in, but all I catch him doing is lying on the bed without having taken off his shoes. He looks up when he notices me and smirks. "Going to join me on the bed? Plenty of room, though I do like to spread out. You might have to sleep on top of me. Or under."

God, he just won't quit. I'm not even dignifying that with an answer.

I kick off my heels. The plush carpet is smooth and soft under my bare feet. Roses and lilies spread in full bloom across the walls, continuing the amazing patterns from the living room. Romantic if, you know, you were actually here for romance. And not stuck here with an idiot stepbrother.

The only real piece of furniture in the bedroom is the bed, but it's huge. White satin sheets, mounds of white pillows, a thick white down comforter. Everything is white. A white lacy canopy, attached to the ceiling, hangs around it, tied back with satin ribbons. Old fashioned, but in a modern way. Any bride would be thrilled to be here.

"Alright, I'm thirsty." Gavin jumps off the bed, miraculously not leaving any stains on the sheets. Rooting in the bar cabinet, he examines the bottles carefully before choosing one. The liquor is so dark it's almost brown. He pauses and arches an eyebrow at me. "You want some?"

"Uh, no. I'll go with water for now."

"Suit yourself." Opening the fridge next to the bar cabinet, he pulls out a bottle of water and tosses it at me. "Think fast."

I catch it. Go me. "Doesn't that stuff cost a fortune?"

"What do you think this is, a motel? For what we're paying I could call that stick-up-his-ass desk jockey up to serve for me." He grins and screws the cork off the bottle, pouring himself a solid dash in a glass tumbler before recorking it and returning it to the cabinet. "So now what? Christen the bed? Or the couches, maybe? Oh, I know!" He grins over a sip of whisky. "We should do it on the balcony."

What? "You do realize that we're not going to fuck, right? And that you're sleeping on that couch in the other room." Boundaries. We need them, ASAP.

He eyes me skeptically. "It's a big fucking bed. Plenty of room for us even without me getting between your legs."

"Couch."

"You're a cruel bitch, Sis." He sighs melodramatically. "But I suppose I knew that."

My train of thought as I try to come up with a reply is interrupted when the ship's horn blows loud enough to make me jump. Three long blasts and then the floor shifts just slightly under my feet. Outside the windows, the city seems like it's moving very slowly. I want to go look, but I don't want to act like a tourist.

Gavin solves it for me. "This is your first time, right? Let's watch." He grabs his tumbler and heads for the balcony.

I don't really want be anywhere near him right now, but I do want to see. I might never be on a luxury cruise ship again, so I follow him outside. It's windy this high up, making me shiver. I should've dug my sweater out of my suitcase, but if I take the time to find it now, I'll miss it.

Gavin sees me shiver and stands behind me. "I'll keep you warm, if you want."

Rolling my eyes, I bite back over my shoulder, "Don't touch me."

He steps back, raising his hands. "Hey, just offering, Sis. It's the kinda stuff big brothers do, right?"

Whatever. I know exactly what kind of brotherly love he has for me, and chivalry has nothing to do with it. Besides, I have a luxury liner departure to watch.

It's not quite like in those old movies with the transatlantic ships setting out and the docks packed with cheering people and streamers, but there're at least a few people down there under the floodlights keeping the dock lit, waving as the ship pulls out. I wave back, though I've no idea who they are. They probably can't see me up here anyway. Gavin throws me an amused glance before looking the other way, towards the open ocean.

As the ship picks up steam, it's not long before the only sounds left are seagulls, water streaming by below us and the rumble of engines deep within the ship. It's beautiful, but watching the shore pull away is a little scary too. There's no running away now.

Gavin drops into a deck chair and sets his drink on the table next to it. The sun set a while ago, and the only light is what streams out from our room, so from my angle he's mostly hidden in darkness.

"You're being unusually quiet. I haven't heard a crude comment in minutes." I sit in the chair across the table from him.

"I dunno. Thinking about this marriage shit."

"If I'm not letting you fuck me, I'm sure as hell not letting you marry me."

He laughs. "We'll see about that. What about you?"

"What about me?" I have lots of feelings about the marriage, most of which I don't intend to share with him.

"What do you think of this whole marriage thing? Your mom's getting hitched to a multimillionaire, if not billionaire. I lost track of how much money he makes a long time ago. That's got to be a little weird for a girl... um... in your situation." He trails off.

Ouch, direct hit. "*In my situation*? And what situation is that exactly?" My eyes shoot daggers at his outline.

"Well, you know... I mean, I guess you're not homeless exactly, but now you're suddenly heading into super rich territory. What do you think you'll get out of it?" He takes a sip. "College money? Fancy clothes? A car?"

That is so far beyond insulting, words almost fail me. "Screw you, Gavin. I can work for my own damn things, if that's what you're so worried about. I've got a free ride to Stanford."

"Fuck, should've known. You're smart *and* sexy. What are you going for?" His question sounds like an inmate's. *What are you in for?*

"Pre-med. I even have a lot of the first year requirements done early."

He laughs, a short bark. "No wonder you're still a fucking virgin."

I consider denying it, but what would be the point? I get up, taking my water and heading for the door when he stops me.

"Wait. I'm just saying, you'd had to have worked real hard for that. Me? I tried business, but dropped out after a few months. I didn't have time for that shit."

I stop in the door, insulted that he thinks education is 'that shit', and annoyed that he has enough money for it not to matter. "Am I supposed to be surprised that a thug like you never graduated college? Hell, I'm surprised you graduated high school." The temperature's dropping as the ship moves further from land, but nowhere near as fast as it does in the space between the two of us.

"Loosen up and enjoy it while you can is my advice. It's not going to fucking last, anyway." He huffs, looking back out over the water.

"What's not going to last?"

"Their marriage. You think this is the first time?"

He drains the last of the whiskey. "This is Dad's fourth marriage, plus a couple of false starts that didn't even get that far. He's a hard man to live with, especially when you're only marrying him for his money."

I'm halfway in, but I storm back out to stand over him. "Are you calling my mom a gold digger?"

He shrugs. "Just saying, isn't it awfully convenient? Her business isn't doing well, right? Are you so goddamn sure?" In the dark, his pupils are black, his eyes rectangular slits under his thick, frowning eyebrows.

I turn away, my voice quieter. "Mom's not like that." Right? She grew up poor, working her way up. Meeting Dad and becoming a Navy wife certainly bought her a lot of security, but she's always worked hard. But now that her business isn't doing that well, would she? It all happened so fast.

"For what it's worth, I believe you." His voice is calmer.

"You do?" I talk to him over my shoulder, not looking.

"You're the stubbornest and proudest girl I've met in my life, babe. That shit came from somewhere." His chair scrapes on the deck as he gets up. "I'm getting another drink."

"I don't think stubbornest is a word." I smile at his praise in spite of myself. Why do I even care about his approval?

"I don't give a fuck."

For a minute there he almost seemed reasonable. "Alright. Fine. So what are you working for, then?"

He looks at me curiously. "Working for? I don't have to. I've already got it."

"Seriously? There's nothing you're burning for? Nothing you want to do?" I give him a disbelieving look. "Just party all the time and be an asshole?"

"Sure. Why not? What choice do I have? Dad expects me to take over at some point, so I guess I will. Maybe I'll just sell it all off when he's gone. Live off the interest." He shrugs.

Must be nice to not care about money. "Sounds boring."

"Hey, it's how the other half lives. You're born. You do what they tell you and have fun while you can until it's over. Are you hungry?"

The conversation just got way too deep. My stomach rumbles in response to the talk about food.

"Hell yeah."

"Alright, I'll order up some room service."

By the time I'm done staring at the water and looking for the horizon in the darkness, the food's here. They're quick. There's so much food you'd think we're having guests. "How many people is this seafood platter for, anyway?"

"Doesn't matter. Eat up. Put some fucking meat on those bones." He grins while cracking a gigantic lobster claw.

"What are you trying to say?"

"That I don't want you to break when you're under me."

I roll my eyes, but crude come-ons are almost a relief. This Gavin I can deal with, even if the thought of him over me makes me tingle. I'm not letting him know that. *I* don't even want to know that. Gavin can dream all he wants, but it'll never be more than that. There's still Paul, if nothing else. "Then I'll eat as little or much as I want, because that'll never happen."

"Maybe not tonight. Maybe not tomorrow night. But some night. And soon." That cocky smirk again.

The stupid thing is that I can't quite keep the smile off my face either. It must be the white wine, or

the chocolates, or the sea air. It's definitely not him.
"In your dreams." I raise my glass to him. "To all
expenses paid luxury cruises."

He raises his, responding with an eloquent,
"Fuck yeah."

8 ANGIE

The rest of the evening, he doesn't mention sex at all. It's like aliens stole the Gavin I know and replaced him with a well-behaved clone. I hate to admit it, but he's actually pretty fun when he's not in asshole-mode. He might not have been college material, but he's done a lot of crazy shit and he's smarter than he acts. Maybe it's more that college wasn't Gavin material. Either way, with all the tension between us, it feels weird to actually have a civilized conversation with him.

"So." He looks at me across the table, looking as stuffed as I feel. "If you could have anything in the world that you wanted, what would it be?"

"Anything?"

"Anything. Absolutely anything. But a thing, not some world peace bullshit or whatever."

I mull it over. Cars, jewelry, designer things. All nice, but I know right away it's none of those. "Old books. I love the smell and feel of them, with the rough cut paper and fancy print. And I'd need a nice bookshelf to keep them in. Maybe one of those fancy libraries that you have in mansions with shelves everywhere and deep leather chairs, know what I mean?"

He eyes me like I was just offered ice-cream and chose broccoli instead. "Books? Seriously? Who's your favorite author?"

I blank. "That's like asking a mom to pick her favorite kid. I don't know, there are so many."

"Pick one."

"Lewis Carroll." I second guess myself right away when I see the look on his face. Too childish? Heinlein? Steele? Nabokov? I don't know. It's not fair to ask me to choose.

Gavin laughs, a short burst. "Alice in Wonderland? Really?"

To be honest, I'm surprised he even knows who Lewis Carroll is. "Really? *You're* a reader?" I'm pretty sure the disbelief comes through clearly in my voice.

"You think I showed up on Earth like this? I was a kid once too you know." He grins. "But I probably just saw the movie."

"Oh whatever. What about you?" Before he answers, I hurry to add, "And for you it can't be something you buy. You can already buy anything you want, so the question's pointless then."

He pauses, thinking, opening his mouth once as if to say something, but doesn't. I arch an eyebrow at him, but he only glowers. "You know what, this is a stupid game. Let's do something else." His eyebrows rise. "We could get naked."

And there we go, the aliens returned the real Gavin. "Not happening, hot shot. Why can't you answer? You owe me. I answered yours."

"I don't owe you squat. Forget the question, alright?"

Wow. Something set him off there. "Fine. Whatever." I don't know why he tries so hard to pretend nothing matters.

"Fine," he mocks.

We both drink, awkwardness filling the air between us like a miasma. I glance at my phone. No new messages, but it's 12:42. No wonder I'm tired.

"Jesus, it's past midnight. I should sleep." We finished off both the champagne and the wine that came with dinner, and I'm definitely feeling it.

"Already?" While I've got a solid buzz going, he seems almost unaffected. "This is when the day gets going."

"For you, maybe. Besides, any more wine, and I might let you do something I'll regret." I roll my eyes at myself. I shouldn't encourage him.

"Yeah?" He grins broadly and makes as if to pour me more.

"Yeah," I laugh, pulling my glass away. "Like let you have a pillow and blanket for the couch, or... talk to me in public." He laughs and pours anyway, letting the wine run onto the tablecloth. I quickly put my glass back just to catch it. "No more. You're crazy, you know that?"

"It may have come up once or twice." He watches me put the glass down and get up. "You're really all done?"

"Told you, I'm going to bed." My head swims as I stand. "Whoa. Yep, straight to bed." I'm not quite falling over drunk, but I'm a cheap date. He was right about one thing at least, studying didn't leave much time for parties. I'm a little proud of myself for not stumbling too much, but when I look back and see his grin, I realize I'm not impressing anyone.

Gavin gets up and follows me to the bedroom. I turn to him and almost fall over. "Why are you following me?"

"Ease up, cupcake. My stuff's in here too." Crouching by his suitcase, he tugs it open.

"Alright, look away. I'm getting under the covers," I announce louder than I need to.

"Why? Do you sleep naked?" He sounds hopeful.

"Nooooooo…" I drag the word out. "But I didn't bring PJs, since I thought I'd be here with my *boyfriend*." He actually flinches at the emphasis I put into it. "So I want you to look away while I strip to my underwear."

To my surprise, he actually turns. "I'm doing this under fucking protest. You're a tease, babe."

"Am not." I slip my clothes off as quickly as I can.

"Are too."

"Am not." I climb onto the bed.

"Nice ass."

Looking back, I find him ogling me with his usual cocky smirk. With a squeal, I rush under the covers, pulling them up to my neck while he laughs. "You said you wouldn't look, you jerk."

"I looked away while you stripped, babe. You didn't say anything about after you were done." He roots around in his suitcase until he finds a pair of pajama pants. "Some of us came prepared."

What I'm not prepared for is him changing right in front of me. Tugging his shirt off, Gavin bares his muscular torso, his dark tattoos stark against his skin. I'm too drunk to hide my interest as I watch him strip. He grins, unbuckling his pants slowly. "You like the show, babe? I'll let you slip in a dollar if you use your teeth."

Heat rushes to my face, and I make a point of turning around. "You'd have to make change, and there's not much to look at anyway."

He only laughs, and I hear his pants hit the floor. "Better hurry if you want to see the main event."

And the stupid thing? I look. I can't help it. Pulling down the comforter just enough to peek, I catch him as he tugs off his black boxer briefs, tossing them onto his pants. Oh my God. He doesn't cover a thing, letting his dick hang out. *Holy crap.*

Not quite as impressive as my first look, but still, wow. He catches me, the corners of his eyes crinkled with amusement. "Looks good enough to eat, right?" Even as I watch, he starts to grow, and all I can do is stare wide-eyed as he gets longer and thicker. Then he tugs his pajamas up. "Show's over, babe. Unless you're up for dessert." He laughs at my frantic head shake and turns to the other room. Stopping in the doorway, he eyes the couch skeptically.

Gavin throws a pleading glance my way, with big puppy dog eyes and a dismay written all over his face. "I'm going to be walking fucking crooked tomorrow from all the kinks I'll get sleeping on that thing."

"Serves you right." I already know it's too short for him, and it's got those wooden armrests. He's not kidding, but seriously? Sharing a bed?

"Fine. Whatever." He still looks like a sad, kicked puppy.

I sigh. This was probably the look mini-Gavin practiced in the mirror before he was old enough to work on his mother-pleasing face. It works, damn him. "Stop. Alright, you can stay. But keep on your side. Don't embarrass yourself."

He looks genuinely relieved. "I know I don't say this often, but you're a fucking gem, Sis." When he turns, it's pretty obvious that his pants don't hide a thing. Still at half mast, his dick bounces freely under the soft fabric, holding my attention in ways I don't want to admit to.

The bed shifts as he sits down and slips under the comforter. I tuck down the sides, wrapping myself in, but even just knowing that he's there creates a kind of intimacy that's hard to ignore.

Jesus, Angie, it's not like you have the hots for him or anything.

Right?

9 ANGIE

Ugh. I'm pretty sure I'm in bed, but everything's rocking. My eyes open slowly, and I look around with bleary eyes. Why does my head hurt so much? What is this place? Is it heaven? Everything's white.

Suddenly it all comes back to me with a crash. The cruise. The wine. Gavin.

Still blinking, I'm convinced something else feels wrong. I shift, or I try to. I'm stuck. Why am I stuck? Drawing a deep breath, I stop and think. It's like swimming to the surface from far underwater. Mornings are never my thing, but hung over, they're apparently even worse.

I'm pinned by an arm, slung over me by a large warm presence that's spooning me. It feels nice. Cozy almost. I'm tempted to close my eyes and slip back to sleep. Of course, the only people in here are me and Gavin, so—

My eyes go wide. Shit. He's supposed to be on his side, not attached to mine. What's he doing wrapped around me? And why does it have to feel so nice? Now that I'm aware of him, I can feel his deep breathing, his chest pressing against my back every time he inhales, and his soft warm breath brushing over my neck when he lets it back out. His muscular arm is heavy, holding me close. I'm lying in a sort of running position, with one leg in front of the other, and one of his legs is across the back one. I'm completely stuck.

He's asleep. Thank God. Maybe he doesn't know. I don't want to wake him, but I'm not sure what to do. I want to stay put, even burrow in deeper against him, but with how things are, that would be a Terrible Idea. But what can I do? It's hard to think when my head feels like I'm wearing a helmet one size too small.

Indecision makes me pause, pausing makes me lower my head to my pillow, and being hung over makes my eyes slide shut. I'll fix it in the morning. Or whenever I wake up. Then all the white fades back to black.

10 GAVIN

Mmm… Nothing like waking up with an almost naked girl in your arms and her sexy ass pressing against your morning wood. I don't usually stick around long enough, but so long as I'm here… except wait, shit. This isn't my place, and that's not where that particular ass is supposed to be. Or I'm supposed to be. Or something.

My eyes pop open, finding wild, dark bed hair sticking in all directions right in front of my face. Angie. Not only is she pressing against my hardon, I've got my arm around her. It also looks like it's decidedly my fault, as I'm about as close to her side of the bed as is possible without pushing her off the bed.

Well, fuck.

I listen and hear her soft steady breathing. At least she's still asleep. My cock twitches, thinking this is awesome, but this isn't my gig. God knows I'd love to fuck her brains out, and if I take it soft and sweet, she might even let me, but when it happens, it's going to be because she wants it, not because I've got her trapped and unconscious. I have my pride. And morals, I guess, but don't let it get around. A guy has a reputation to maintain.

Alright, easy does it. I try to slide away, but she's grabbed onto my arm, which is fucking cute and all, but doesn't make it any easier to pull away. Still, she's a heavy sleeper, and with a little tug I get my arm loose. Then it's just a matter of rolling away carefully.

It's when I immediately run out of comforter that I understand how I ended up on her end of the bed. Self-preservation. The little blanket thief. Most of it's hanging over the edge and down on the floor on the other side of her. I've probably just been chasing her across the mattress in my sleep, trying to stay warm. So nothing happened.

No harm, no foul. Unfortunately.

I grab my phone from the nightstand. Almost eleven. Man, we've slept in. Good thing we don't have a schedule. Throwing my legs over the edge of the bed, I gather my will before pushing myself to my feet. Mornings suck, my mouth tastes like cotton and I need a shower.

That, and my hardon's refusing to die down.

I close the door to the bathroom quietly so I don't wake her. A quick brushing of the teeth, one really awkward leak since I'm still hard as rock, and then into the shower. Fuck, I need one like this at home. It's fucking huge, and the pressure's the kind that peels the dirt right off your back. We're fucking millionaires. Why do I have a crappy shower?

As soon as the hot water hits my back, I forget about it. The shower fills with steam and the hot water pounds down my back, relaxing every muscle in my body. Well, apart from one. Apparently my cock's pissed I didn't get my morning fix, and has decided it needs attention. Since the odds of getting Angie's help in the immediate future are pretty fucking slim, I guess I'm fisting it. Not as much fun as with a little help, but a man's got to do what a man's got to do.

Immediately, my mind tries to imagine how this morning might've gone had Angie actually been interested. And naked. Definitely naked. The swell of her gorgeous tits is already burned into my mind from that first night. I only got a glimpse of her smooth pussy before she bailed on me, but that glimpse will stick with me for the rest of my life, along with the view of her rounded ass and the slope of her sexy back I left behind only minutes ago.

I close my eyes and remember the brief taste I had of her soft lips. Nice and plump, they'd look good wrapped around my cock, sliding up and down the length of it in time with my fist. The warm hollow of her mouth. The wet touch of her tongue along the underside. Oh, Jesus.

I stroke faster, my body tensing up as I approach the point of no return. Images of Angie on her knees in front of me and working me with that pouty little mouth flash over the backs of my eyelids. My calves tighten, bringing me up on my toes as I work myself harder and faster. I feel the boiling in my balls, and my cock swells in my hand. And that's of course just the moment the door opens.

The point of no return flashes by, and my cock explodes, shooting thick streams against the glass shower door, one after another. Just on the other side, Angie's wide eyes stare at me in shock, but there's nothing I can do. I pulse over and over until just a dribble seeps out the end, the shower door between us plastered with translucent white trails.

Oh fuck me.

She's frozen in place, but finally finds her voice. "Oh God, I'm so sorry! I wasn't—I just needed a glass of water, and—I'll close the door." She slams it shut.

Yeah. So sorry. Awesome.

I hose down the door with the showerhead, rinse myself clean and shut the water off. I dry myself slowly, dreading going back out there. If my brain had been working enough, I should've invited her in to help clean up, but it's too late for witty one liners. Like relations weren't bad enough already, now there's going to be an ice front worthy of the fucking Cold War.

Talk about something coming between us.

Maybe I should just go out there naked, it's not like she hasn't seen the whole show by now. That might shut her up. Except I just came, so I'm feeling good. Embarrassed, but good. Pulling my pajama pants on, I take a deep sigh before opening the door, prepared to face the music. I'm sure this will be awesome.

Angie's in bed, rolled away from me, her shoulders shaking. Fuck, is she actually crying? What the hell am I supposed to say to that? "Listen. Angie. I'm sorry." Why the fuck am I sorry? She's the one who burst in on me.

Her shoulders heave. That seems over the top. Did I hit some sort of trigger or something?

"Gavin…" Her voice is strained.

Drawing a deep breath, I wait for it. She snorts. Hold on, is she—

That's not fucking crying. "Angie…" I put all the menace I can into my tone and she loses it.

It explodes out of her, peals of laughter rushing out like a burst water main. I'd call it musical, but it's so out of control and raw. It'd be fucking cute if it wasn't at my expense. It's so bad, she rolls over onto her back and beats the sheets with her fists and wheezes for air.

"Oh God." She barely gets it out between breaths. "You should—you should see your face right now."

For fuck's sake, it wasn't *that* funny. Can't a guy have a little private time without it turning into comedy hour? "What, and you don't take care of business, babe? Didn't you hear the fucking shower?"

For a moment she stops, staring at me with those big brown eyes, her lips pinched tightly. The corners of her lips are pulling up, as if she's just barely hanging on. She shakes her head no. She snorts, then loses it again.

Completely out from under the covers and sprawling across the bed, I don't think she realizes how amazingly fuckable she looks right now in only her bra and panties. It takes a lot of a willpower to not jump up on the bed and throw myself down between her legs. *That* would shut her up. Instead, I roll my eyes and pretend to look for something in my suitcase so she won't see me stiffening up. In this mood she'd probably just laugh, and my pride can only take so much fucking abuse.

While I'm rooting around, Angie seems to quiet down. Maybe she's finally done.

She snorts.

Or not.

"Enough already. I fucking get it. Watching me jerk off is fucking hilarious. Are we fucking done yet?"

She sits up, biting down on her lower lip. Lifting her hands, balled up into fists, right in front of her she pushes out at me while spreading her fingers wide. "Splooosh!" Then she throws herself at the bed, losing it again.

Alright. That's it. I've fucking had it. She wants to act like a kid? I'll show her what happens to bad little girls. Two quick steps and I leap onto the bed. She looks up in confusion, but doesn't have enough time to do anything before I pick her up. Fuck, she's so light.

"What are you doing? Put me down, you perv!" She doesn't know whether to be mad or laugh, and does a little of both, still giggling while her eyes spark angrily.

"Only doing what I should've done a long time ago." Sitting down at the edge of the bed, I throw her over my lap, face down and cheeks up. Fuck, that's fine. Putting my left arm across her back to keep her in place, I put my right hand right on the perkiest ass I've ever had my hands on. Her smooth skin is warm and soft underneath my palm.

She wriggles, trying to get loose. "Get your hands off me!" She's not laughing quite so hard anymore.

I don't answer. Lifting my hand dramatically, I bring it down with a loud smack. Her soft flesh quivers, making me want to sink into her from behind and watch. She looks so fucking sexy like that.

"Ow! What the fuck?"

I smack her again, watching her ass jiggle. "Just a little lesson in respect, Sis."

"What? Fuck you!"

"Rule number one, when the bathroom door's closed, it means it's busy. Were you raised in a fucking barn?"

Smack.

Her ass reddens a little. "Ow! Jesus, Gavin, I was half asleep, alright. I didn't even think about it." She tries to get loose, but I'm too strong for her.

"Rule number two, when you catch a guy at his most vulnerable, you do *not* make fun of him." I've never really done this before, but I'm getting into this rules and discipline shit.

Smack.

She's not squirming as much as she was, I can feel her body starting to submit. "You're not liking this, are you?" I laugh and bring my hand down again, loving the soft give of her tender flesh.

Smack.

"Fuck you... Gavin." Her breath's coming heavier, and she's not struggling at all now.

Seriously? That's all it takes? I really should've done this earlier.

"Oh, Sis. I keep offering, but you keep saying no."

I smack her again, letting my hand rest on the curve of her ass, right where the line of her panties cuts across her sexy cheek. She actually lets out a soft little moan. My cock never really went down all the way, but now blood's rushing into it like it's got a hot date, and suddenly in spite of the shower, I'm rock hard. She has to feel me pressing against her stomach, but she's suspiciously quiet.

"And rule number three, don't tease a guy if you're not gonna go through with it."

Smack.

Letting my hand trail along her curve, I slide it in between her legs. I expect her to clamp her legs together, but she doesn't. She just lies in my lap, breathing heavily. Her panties are soaked. Holy shit. Pushing my fingers against her heat through the thin fabric, I rub gently, making her moan again, louder this time.

"That feel good, babe?" She's so soft. And I'm so fucking hard.

"I'm not... your babe." Her protest is half-hearted.

Angie's writhing on my lap like a cat in heat. My hot little pussy. I knew she had it in her, and I want to rip those panties off and fuck her silly, but any wrong moves and she'll bolt. So instead, I keep stroking her softly through her wet panties.

Her ass wriggles against my hand, like she's trying to capture my fingers. She fists the sheets, body tense. Every breath is a quiet moan now as she gets more and more worked up.

I'm just about to risk sliding my hand under the elastic so I can get my skin right on hers when someone knocks on the door. She stiffens, while I try to ignore it. "Sssh, babe."

The knock comes again. "Mr. Caldwell, Sir?"

Oh, for fuck's sake. "What is it?"

"Important message for you, Sir." The voice is a little squeaky, as if its owner's voice is still changing.

"Let go of me." I look down to find Angie looking back up over her shoulder, her tone measured and even. "Let me go." I can't read her eyes. Her face is flushed and she doesn't seem angry, but confused, maybe?

The moment's ruined anyway, so I let up. She slides quickly out of my lap and wraps the comforter around herself, like she's suddenly embarrassed to be seen in her underwear. Fuck, innocence isn't usually my thing, but she's sexy when she blushes.

"Sir?" Right. The guy at the door.

Angie looks right at me. "Shouldn't you get that?"

11 ANGIE

Gavin gets up and adjusts himself to hide the huge bulge in his pants. The memory of it pressing against my stomach while he was spanking me… *spanking* me flashes through my mind and without thinking about it, I put a hand against the spot where it rubbed.

His hands, his cock, the memory of their touch feels branded into my skin. He was in full control. I'd been completely at his mercy, and I'd loved it. But it's Gavin. Asshole, stepbrother, playboy. *Not my boyfriend.* I don't want to need him like that. He'd chew up my heart and spit it out. Except I can think that all I want, but it doesn't make me any less wet.

Crap.

I throw on one of my beach wraps like a robe

and go see who's at the door. Gavin's standing there looking like raw sex and pissed to be interrupted. Next to him, the steward at the door looks like a kid playing dress up in an oversized sailor suit.

"Good morning, Sir. I sincerely hope I didn't disturb you," The steward manages to squeak out.

Gavin snorts. "You did. What do you want?"

The kid swallows. "I was asked by the captain to bring you this message." He hands over a silver plate with a card on it. "It's an invitation for you and your lovely fiancée to join Captain Melbourne at his table for dinner tonight."

My eyes widen at that. At the captain's table? That sounds fancy, and I mostly brought bikinis and t-shirts. Crap. "Gavin, tell him we can't—"

"Thank you. Please tell the captain we'd be honored." Gavin's reply is silky smooth. He sounds like his dad, all wealth and courtesy. It suits him. But it's also the wrong answer.

"Gavin—"

The steward continues, "He also asked me to let you know that all arrangements are in place for Sunday, just as you requested."

"Arrangements?" Gavin runs a hand through his

messy hair, sounding as confused as I am.

"Yes, Sir. For…" He trails off, then nods his head in my direction as if I can't see it. "The arrangements, Sir. At 6:00 PM on Sunday."

I still don't think Gavin gets it. I know I don't, but he nods. "Right. Of course. Tell Captain Melbourne thank you, and that we'll join him for dinner tonight. At what time?"

"Oh, I'm sorry, it's at eight, Sir."

"Excellent. Write yourself a tip for the favor and put it on this room. A hundred bucks."

The steward's eyes go wide just like mine do, but to his credit his mouth doesn't drop open, unlike mine. For all I know, that's standard tipping fare on a ship like this, but I suspect not. "Thank you, Sir. That's very generous."

"Consider it a deposit on leaving a fucking note next time. You got me?" Gavin, apparently done with keeping up appearances, shuts the door in his face and turns to me. "Dinner with the captain, huh?"

"Gavin!" I hiss, clutching my wrap around me. "I don't have anything to wear. And a hundred bucks in tip?"

"That's alright. I think you look great in what

you've got on, to be honest. Unless I can talk you out of it." He grins, crossing his thick arms over his chest and leaning up against the liquor cabinet.

The heat of my blush rushes to my face, my thoughts suddenly back on being over his knee and his fingers probing my... "I'm serious! I didn't bring clothes for a fancy dinner. I was figuring on living on buffets and fruity drinks while I lounged by the pool."

He looks at me curiously, like he doesn't get the problem. "Alright. So we'll pick some up then. There's plenty of shopping on board."

A couple days ago I was worrying about not having a summer job so I could buy books and gas money. If I could afford designer clothes I wouldn't have a Charlie's Chicken application on my desk back home. "Are you insane? I can't afford to buy new clothes, especially here, where they probably double the prices."

He laughs. "Probably triple, at least. But, babe. You can afford it."

I'm sick of his babe shtick, but I let it go because it's by far not my biggest problem. "Afford it? Did I win the lottery or something?"

He tilts his head and looks at me like I'm an

idiot. "No, but your mom did."

"Okay, for starters, no matter what it says on the ticket, *I'm not my mom.* And also? They're not even married yet."

"Close enough. I'll cover it, and if you feel really guilty, I do accept sexual favors in currency. Come on."

I follow him back to the bedroom, sputtering in indignation. Facing his suitcase and away from me, he drops his pants, letting them fall to his ankles before he steps out of them. My mouth dries up and my arguments fade. Oh my God, that ass. Tight and dimpled, it's made for grabbing. The curved end of a tattoo twines down over the right side, and I feel jealous of the needle that got to do it.

He turns his head and catches me watching. "If you're gonna stare at me like that, I'm going to add it to your tab. I really should get something in return for all this generosity." The smirk is back. He's a cocky asshole. I just wish he wasn't such a good-looking cocky asshole. "You'll get this one for free," he quips over his shoulder, "But I'm not going to stand for it for long. Consider yourself warned, babe." Then he pulls on underwear and pants, and the show's over.

He must by wearing me down, because instead of getting angry, I actually laugh. It's possible that there actually is a nice guy under that horn dog act. So just to play with him, I drop my wrap, grab clean clothes and stroll into the bathroom to change. It's not like he hasn't seen me anyway, right?

When I come back out, he makes a show of looking me up and down before he opens the door and gestures gallantly. "After you, my lovely fiancée." I roll my eyes and step past him. At least it wasn't babe.

12 GAVIN

"Holy crap, Gavin. We can't buy this!" Angie looks at me with those big doe eyes. "Can we?"

Shopping with Angie has been an experience. This is the first girl I've been with who I had to drag away from the clearance racks and force to look at the good stuff. Right now, she's wearing one sexy as hell red Roberto Cavalli dress that hangs off one shoulder and makes her look like a fucking movie star. Standing in front of one of the full length mirrors, she's lifting the light-as-feather fabric and twisting back and forth like Cinderella, watching herself as if she can't quite believe it's true.

The dress costs so much that ruining it by fucking her in it sounds blasphemous, but right now that's exactly what I want to do. Chase the store clerks out and fuck her silly right over that counter.

I try not to say that part out loud. "Stop worrying, babe. Every eye's gonna be on you tonight. You look good enough to fuck." Oh well, I tried.

Angie looks at me in shock, her face darkening with embarrassment. The clerks are professional enough to let it pass with just brief raising of their brows, but I'm sure they'll be gossiping about it afterwards. I don't give a fuck. She *does* look that good.

"Gavin!" She's trying to look mad, but I can tell she's pleased. At least the part of her that isn't dying of embarrassment.

I should leave her alone, but she's cute when she's flustered. I step up close behind her and put my hands on her hips. "I just love you so much, babe. Just imagine, once we're married we can do it every day." That I said loud enough for the sales people to hear, but then I lean in, my mouth right by her ear and whisper, "I'm ready to start tonight, and I have a very, *very* active imagination."

"Gavin!" Her voice just went up an octave. Even the clerks are having a hard time pretending disinterest. Fuck, she's so fun to tease.

Show's over. Any more of this and I will be fucking her in the shop. "We'll take it. Just pack it up and deliver it to our room, please." I address the clerks, who nod eagerly, commissions ringing up in their eyes.

"Excellent choice, Sir."

I turn to Angie. "Want me to come into the changing room with you and help you get off? Get it off, I mean. You know, the dress."

There's ice in that gaze, but it was worth it. "No, thank you, Gavin. I'll manage."

"Just offering." I can't keep the grin off my face, while the salesgirls watch our exchange with interest.

We continue store hopping. Black Rodarte shoes. A Cartier white gold and diamond necklace with orchid shapes that looks fantastic around her graceful neck. We're just coming out of the Annick Goutal store when she stops me. "Gavin. Stop."

"Stop what?"

"This. How much money are you spending on me? You haven't let me see the totals, but I know it has to be crazy. We can't buy all these things." For a moment she puts her hands on my arm before I glare at her and she pulls back like she's burned them.

I'm sick of her second guessing me. It's fun to watch her get so excited, but it's a pain in the ass to keep reassuring her. "Babe. You're supposed to be my fiancée. Unlike you, I packed a suit, and it's the real deal. If we're going to sit with the captain, I'm not letting you embarrass me in some shit you put together like you wore to that cheap-ass club."

The expression on her face is like I just slapped her. She goes from anxious and humble to killing me with her eyes. Viciously and painfully. "You're an asshole, you know that?"

"It's been mentioned. But come on, you love it, right?" I wonder if maybe I went a little overboard, because I see hurt behind the fury.

"No. I don't freaking love it. I can't believe you." She raises a finger and points it right at my chest. I'm in deep shit, but she's fucking gorgeous when she's angry. "Every once in a while, I start to suspect that there's a real human being underneath that cocky, arrogant, asshole exterior that you like to show. Then you remind me of who you really are, a spoiled little rich boy who hasn't had to work for a single thing in his life."

People are staring. I bet this isn't great for our reputation as happy soon-to-be-weds on a pleasure cruise before the big event. She's not done though, advancing until her finger actually jabs right into my chest. "You know what? Forget it. I'm sick of your designer things, your pervy jokes and your daddy's money. You think you're so much better than me? This isn't even yours. You couldn't hack your own thing so you're just riding on daddy's coattails. I'm done."

She turns her back and storms away, leaving me to stare after her like an idiot. What went wrong? That went way beyond our usual back and forth. I tell her to stop worrying about money, and she throws the one personal thing I've shared with her back in my face? Fuck that. I should go after her and settle this, right here, right now, but I'm too pissed. I'll do something I'll regret.

Whatever. Maybe she isn't any different from all those other girls after all. Sugary sweet when she wants to be, and then she turns on a fucking dime as soon as she gets a whiff of something she doesn't like. Well now I know, but we're still stuck together.

Fuck. There's got to be a good bar around here

somewhere. A place serving something strong enough to wipe that look of hurt in her eyes from my mind.

13 ANGIE

Why does he have to be such a jerk? I mean, sometimes he's funny. Even sexy. But then he turns around and says shit like that. Logically I understand he didn't know the dress I had on that night was the only decent one I own, but to have it rubbed in my face?

I rush up the stairs where there are less people. There's the elevator, but waiting means standing still, and I can't stand still right now. I need to walk it off. I'm sure as hell not going back to our room.

I see a door labeled AFT DECK 1 and I take it, emerging outside. It was nice earlier, but now the skies have clouded up, which suits my mood perfectly. Maybe that's why there are so few people out here. That's just fine.

The deck is nearly empty as I charge to the very back of the ship where I can be alone, watching the massive wake of the cruise ship spread behind us. Why do I let him get to me so badly? His opinion doesn't matter. I don't even like him. In fact, I'm starting to think I fucking hate him.

With all that's been going on, I haven't even given a thought to Paul. It makes me feel guilty to think of how easily I accepted that he wasn't coming. I didn't even call. Of course, he didn't call me, either.

Argh, men! I should've brought Cassie. We'd have found a way, ID or no ID.

My phone rings, and when it starts playing Wild Thing, I actually freak out a little. It's Cassie, as if thinking about her has summoned her to me in my time of need. Thank God, because I could totally deal with a friendly voice right now. I hit the button.

"Hello?"

"Angie! Where the hell are you? You dropped off the face of the planet and no one knows where you are."

Shit, I should've sent her a message or something. "I'm sorry. I'm on a cruise."

There's silence on the other end for a few moments. "You're on a what? A cruise?"

I laugh at her confusion. "Yeah. Some super luxury thing. My new dad tried to give it to Mom, but she gets crazy seasick, so being the disgustingly rich maniac that he is, he tossed the tickets in the trash. I grabbed them, and here I am, stuck with my asshole stepbrother."

"Your new what? Seasick? Asshole stepbrother? Angie, you're not making any sense."

Awesome, I'm a horrible friend in addition to being a horrible girlfriend. She doesn't know anything about Herbert's proposal, or Gavin or any of that. I bring her up to date as quickly and concisely as I can.

When I finish, the silence at the other end is so long that I worry I've lost contact. When she finally speaks, her voice is incredulous. "If it was anyone else but you, Angie, I'd call bullshit. That doesn't happen to anyone."

"Yeah, I know. I'm not sure I'd believe me either, but now I've got this dinner with the captain tonight where I'm going to have to pretend to be not only civil, but in love with my nemesis." I sigh. How the hell am I going to do that?

To my surprise, instead of supporting me, Cassie cracks up. She just won't stop laughing. "God, Angie, do you have any idea about how crazy this sounds? You know what? I think you should go for it."

"What?" I shake my head even though she can't see me. "What do you mean?"

She laughs again. "Come on, I only saw him for like three minutes, but he's crazy hot. Do him. You guys have the freaking bridal suite, a big bed and all the time to yourselves that you want. What happens on the cruise stays on the cruise." She pauses a moment. "And imagine the story. You fucked your stepbrother. Who's he going to tell?"

I huff. "You don't know him. He'll tell everyone, because he's an asshole and doesn't give a shit. He'll probably put it in his Christmas card just for fun. No freaking way. Besides, Paul. Hello." Actually screw him? Is she insane? I swear it's just the cool ocean air making my nipples hard.

"About that." Her voice turns serious. "I had a reason for calling. You just managed to completely derail me. Though now that I know what you're up to, maybe it can wait until you're back. Don't want to mess with your cruise."

I roll my eyes. "Spill. You can't say something like that and not tell me."

She doesn't even hesitate. "Okay, here goes. Yesterday morning, someone kicked the shit out of Paul. He had to get stitches. I'm kind of surprised he hasn't called you to let you know."

What the heck? I can put together two and two as well as anyone, and it doesn't take much to guess at who might be responsible. My blood begins to boil. Not only is Gavin being an asshole, he's gone and sent the guy who's supposed to be my boyfriend to the ER. I knew he was moody and rude, but violent? As much as I hate him at the moment, I have a hard time believing he'd do something like that over a bad case of blue balls.

"Hello? Are you still there?"

"Yeah. Sure. Still here. Do you know anything about why?" There has to be a reason at least, right? Something?

"I couldn't tell you, Ange. Word is, someone busted in on Paul and then kicked his ass. No one knows exactly why, at least that I've spoken to." I can almost hear her shrug over the phone. "No idea. Listen, I've got to go. Keep me posted, alright?"

"Yeah, sure. Will do." I draw a deep breath. "Thanks." I tap the phone, hanging up.

Okay. Now what? I'm apparently rooming with a violent maniac, who's going to be step-related to me and wants to get in my pants. How much worse can this get?

"Why so glum, dearie?" Someone else has braved the gloom to come to share the view, and I didn't even notice. I look up and find one of the old ladies from reception. Jane? Julie? Joyce.

I shake my head. "You wouldn't understand." How could anyone comprehend this mess?

"Try me." She looks frail, but her voice is firm, maybe even a little offended. "You don't think I've been around the block a few times? You don't get this old by *not* living, kid." She snorts.

"Sorry. Rough day." I look back out at the water.

"Husband trouble." She nods at my astonished look. "I've been there. I've had four of them."

Part of me wants to burst out and tell her the whole thing, but what if she goes and tells someone? I'll play it safe. "He's not my husband yet." I flash a smile. "Not ever, if he keeps this up."

"Oh dear, that does sound horrible. Give him

some time." She smiles. "But not too much. Too much, and you kick him out on his ass, dearie." Turning back towards the water, she examines the horizon while I look at her with shock. "But you need to talk to him. Trust me. I know what I'm talking about."

I have a hard time concealing a laugh. "Alright, so how do I know when it's too much?"

She shrugs. "When the thought of tearing his clothes off and making up doesn't feel worth the trouble. And the good ones are always trouble, bless their jackass hearts." Making as if to leave, she turns. "I have to make sure Mabel's not up to anything. Most likely, she's waiting at the lunch buffet."

I watch her go, old and hunched over, but with steady steps. "Thanks for the advice." I think.

She waves briefly. "Of course, dearie. Remember. If he doesn't make you tingle, then out he goes. Now go talk to him. Life's too short for useless husbands." She gives me a little wink. "But if he's a good fuck, give him a chance. Make-up sex is worth a few tears." And with that, she walks off, leaving me speechless. Did she really just say that?

I'm still blinking when she opens the door into

the ship and disappears. I can't tell if she's off her rocker or brilliant. Either way, she's probably got a point. Gavin might not actually be my husband-to-be, but I'm going to have to deal with him for the rest of the cruise.

With a sigh, I go to find him. Like it or not, he does make me tingle.

14 ANGIE

It takes an hour of scouring the ship, but eventually I find him in one of the many bars onboard. The ship is like a miniature floating city, but cleaner. Why it needs that many bars for one ship I have no idea, but they all have themes. Like the one I tracked him down in. It has an old timey western feel. The sort of theme park Wild West that probably never existed outside movies. Saloon doors, a long bar and a burly bartender who looks like he's about to spit in the glass he's holding to wash it.

Gavin's off in a corner, nursing something golden amber that probably isn't apple juice.

I slide into the chair across from him. "Howdy pardner."

He looks up, his hazel eyes glassy. "Did you remember something else to bitch at me about, or just couldn't stay away?"

The bitter tone in his voice makes me wince, because he isn't far off. Is it possible I actually managed to hurt him? I push aside the guilt. He probably doesn't deserve it. "Sober up. I need you to answer something, and for once can you just be honest with me?"

Waiting for him to straighten up, I put my elbows on the table and lean my chin on my hands. Even buzzed, he's hot as hell, his t-shirt painted on him, showing every ridge and edge of his chiseled physique. Joyce's advice rattles around uncomfortably in my brain, but I'm not ready to forgive and forget.

Maybe he actually realizes that I'm serious, since he sits up and blinks away the booze fog. With a frown, he watches me intently. "Alright. I'm listening."

That went almost too easily. "Did you know cell phones work here? I had no idea."

"Of course they do. All of these ships have cell service. They have indoor plumbing and Wi-Fi too, but I guess that's not what you're here to tell me about, though I appreciate the public service announcement." One of his eyebrows arches just barely.

"I was just on the phone with Cassie."

"Is that supposed to mean something to me?"

"The girl who set us up that... night." The Incident. Even now I can't keep heat from flushing my face when I remember.

"The one with the slut phone?"

It takes a second before I realize what he's talking about. "Yeah, her," I reply with a little smile. "She told me something, but I'm not sure I understand. I'm pretty sure it's about you."

"Me?"

"And Paul." I lock my eyes to his expecting... something, but he meets them with no reservations. "Yesterday."

"Ah." He doesn't look away.

"Yeah. Ah. What the hell happened, Gavin?" I lean forward, looking for a shred of remorse. Regret. Something. "Why did Cassie tell me someone kicked his ass yesterday? Probably right around the time you were there."

He shrugs. "Probably because I kicked his ass

yesterday."

Of all the freaking nerve! "Why the hell would you do that? It's not like you couldn't just buy a ticket with your pocket change. Was it just to mess with me? That's over the top, even for you."

Gavin's eyes flash and he leans in so close that our noses almost touch. "You think so? Let me ask *you* something, then. What's Paul's girlfriend's name?" His eyes look huge, filling my vision. Dark and stormy, they draw me in.

"That's a stupid question." I say it real slow. "Angie. Do you want me to spell it for you?"

He laughs, but there's no humor in it. "No, the other one."

"What other one?"

"Violet." He sneers, one side of his lip lifting in a grimace like he just stepped in something.

What the hell? Who's Violet? "Who?"

"You know, his girlfriend. The one he was fucking when I came looking for him. Her name was Violet. Real pretty. Huge fucking tits. They jiggled back and forth so hard while he laid into her I thought she was gonna smack herself in the face."

I want to believe he's joking, but his face is like

stone, dead serious. "I don't believe you."
Unfortunately, I do, but I don't want to. I refuse to.
"And wait, they were fucking? Did you break into
their bedroom or something? How batshit crazy are
you?"

"Hey, I rang the fucking doorbell. Not my fault
she screamed *come in*. Or maybe it was *I'm coming*, now
that I think about it. They were coked out of their
minds, either way."

"What?"

"Did he ever offer to share? It's the least he
could do when you share him with Violet, and who
the fuck knows who else."

"Coke? Like—" He can't possibly be saying what
I think he is.

"White powder. Usually you snort it off a mirror.
Fucks you up. Disgusting shit."

"He doesn't do—" I said I wanted honest, but I
didn't want this. This is too much.

"Of course not. It was probably just Violet's and
he had to hold it for her." He leans back with a shrug,
but his face shows what he really thinks.

"I see." I don't know what to say, or think. Paul
wouldn't do something like that. Sure, he's rough

around the edges, but drugs? Other women? I'm the only one he wants, right? He said so. And Gavin would totally say stuff like this just to get a rise out of me.

Emotion bubbles up, lumping up in my throat. I was going to let Paul be my first. That's why I ran away from Gavin in the first place. Why I couldn't do it. What a hypocrite I am. I was *this* close to having sex with Gavin. Is that much better?

I'm getting angry. I can feel it, but I don't know who to aim it at. Paul, myself, Gavin? Is he telling the truth, or is this just another try at manipulating me? With a glare, I snap, "I don't believe you."

"Call him." He's dead calm.

"Alright." Yeah. I'll call his bluff. "I will." Pulling out my phone, I tap Paul's name. His icon is a little red heart, which makes me wince. Gavin's lying. I know he is.

I know he isn't.

The phone rings forever. Come on, pick up. I know you're there, Paul. It just keeps ringing. Maybe he's busy. This is stupid. What am I even going to say? Meanwhile, Gavin swirls the liquid in his glass, making no sign of backing down.

I'm just about to hang up when there's an answer. "Hello?" The voice is unclear, slow and decidedly female.

"Who's this?" Not the most polite way to start a phone call, but I'm past polite.

"It's Violet. Duh. Who're you?"

"*Duh.* Angie. Paul's *girlfriend.*" I leave the, "you bitch," unsaid. For now.

Her voice is muffled as she screams to someone else in the room. "There's some bitch on the phone saying she's your girlfriend. You wanna explain that shit?" There's a mumbled reply that I can't make out, and then she's back on the line, her voice so caustic I'm surprised it doesn't melt my ear right off. "I don't know who the hell you think you are, but stay the fuck away from Paul." I don't think she spits, but it wouldn't surprise me. The last thing I hear before the line goes dead is, "Crazy-ass bitch."

I almost throw my phone across the bar. The tears come before I can stop them. I don't know if I'm sad or just angry. Probably both, or maybe there's just a limit to how much anyone can be expected to take in a twenty-four hour period and I just passed it. Resting my arms on my elbows and my face in my hands, I sob right there at the table. Crap, I don't want to do this in public.

"Come here." His voice is unusually gentle as Gavin takes my hand and pulls me toward him, around the table. I don't know why I let him. He's my asshole stepbrother, but right now I just want comfort, and he's offering it. Drawing me right into his lap, he wraps his arms around me and holds me close. No teasing. No bullying. Just holding.

"I'm still mad at you, you know," I tell him between sniffles. Wait a minute. I look up at him through itchy, watery eyes. "Why were you even there? Why'd you beat him up?"

Gavin laughs, and I can feel the rumble in his chest. "I know Paul. I know what kind of shit he's up to. I just didn't know he was *your* Paul until the other night." He wrinkles his nose. "You have shitty taste in guys, babe."

That's totally what I want to hear. I push off him. "Thanks for reminding me. You're so right."

"You little brat," he laughs. Instead of letting me go, he pulls me closer. I try to get away, but he's too strong.

I drop back into his lap with grunt. "Let me up,

you bully."

He only laughs at me. "Guilty as charged. I could punch guys in the face for you all night long. Just line them up for me."

I don't even know if that's sweet or just disturbing. "You're a psycho."

"I do what's necessary. I only meant to tell him to back off. He's the one who jumped me when I asked about you. No idea what he was thinking." He arches an eyebrow. "Must've been the fucking coke."

Jesus. "You didn't consider something crazy, like calling the cops? Or telling me? Rather than beating the shit out of him? Sorry, that's psycho reasoning."

"Told ya, he threw the first punch. I was just gonna warn him." He shrugs. "And tell him not to bother showing up, of course."

"Of course." Part of me really enjoys sitting here in his lap, much as I hate to admit it. He's nice and warm, his strong arms wrapped protectively around me. On the other hand, he's Gavin. "Are you going to let me up?"

"Nah."

"Excuse me?" I look at him incredulously, daring him to repeat that.

"Nope. For once we aren't arguing, and I like you right here. Your sexy little body rubbing against me, your sexy round ass grinding against my cock." Even as he says it, I feel his bulge swelling under me. "The fact that I can look right down your shirt."

Pulling the top of my shirt close to my body, I struggle against him. "Let. Me. Go!"

Surprisingly, he lets me up. "Fine. But you're missing out."

"I'm sure you can find someone to take care of you. That's what guys do, isn't it?" I glare at him. "You know, fuck around."

"We aren't all Paul, babe." For a second his face softens. "Look, I'm sorry if something I said pissed you off, but I'm not sorry for fucking up Paul, and I'm not sorry he isn't the one here right now."

That was a sideways sort of non-apology, but it was more than I'd expected, and given the situation, I'd take it. "Yeah, well. I'm sorry if *maybe* I might have overreacted. You might not be quite as vile as I implied."

"Oh, Sis, I knew you cared. Just save some of that that love for dinner tonight. 'Cause we're gonna have to be all romantic and lovey dovey and shit.

Unless you want to get put on land at the nearest port for sneaking aboard."

He shrugs, like he couldn't care less what happens. Which he probably doesn't, because he could charter a jet to go home and leave me to hitchhike if he wanted. But he wouldn't. I want to hate him, but I can't, not anymore. 'Like' might be too strong a word, but… tingles.

I sigh. "Yeah, I'll be there. I'll even pretend to not be repulsed by you."

"Aww, I can't wait." Leaning back with his hands behind his head, he smiles broadly at me. "I expect a lot of making out, babe."

"I'm sure you do," I say sweetly. "But you know, with my chastity vows and all, we're going to have to keep things decent until we're actually married." I blink at him innocently. "I'd hate to go back on my vows now that we're so close."

He actually laughs out loud. "We'll see, babe. We'll see."

I turn to leave, then stop again. "Thanks."

Sitting up, he give me a confused look. "For what?"

"For kicking Paul's ass. You're a Neanderthal,

but nobody's ever done something like that for me, so... thanks." I shrug. "You're almost acting like a real big brother, or something."

He grins mischievously. "Does that mean we'll fuck tonight?"

"I think you missed the 'big brother' part, perv." This time I do walk off, calling over my shoulder, "See you at dinner."

15 ANGIE

I've just returned to our suite when the punchy beat of Momma Said Knock You Out bursts out of my phone. Great, now I have to explain where I am. I tap the phone and put it to my ear. "Hey, Mom."

"Angela! Where have you been? I haven't seen you since yesterday morning. I've been worried sick." Her normally calm voice quavers, which seems over the top. It's not like I haven't been gone overnight before.

I keep my voice steady. "I'm fine. I've been over at Cassie's. Paul and I broke up. I just needed some girl time, ya know? Is everything alright? You could've called if you were worried." It feels cheap using something that just happened as emotional leverage, but she'll never question a brokenhearted sleepover.

"Oh, honey…" She sounds sad for me, and I feel guilty for misleading her. "Take all the time you need. Things have been so busy lately. I'm sorry I haven't been paying more attention. I just wanted to know you're alright."

"Yeah, Mom, I'm fine, promise." It's at that moment the ship's horn blasts loudly, scaring the crap out of me.

"Honey, what was that? Are you down at the docks?"

"Uh… no, we're just watching Titanic. You know. Chick movies, popcorn, PJs, the whole thing." I think we did that once. That's believable, right?

"Alright, you know that's not a very good neighborhood." She sounds suspicious, but not for the right reasons. "I don't want to spoiler or anything, but the ship goes down." We groan together.

"Thanks a lot, Mom. Now we'll have to watch something else." We laugh together too. "So anyway, I'm safe and sound, watching movies so old DiCaprio looks young, and everything's okay. Was that it?"

"Actually, there is something else." She sounds excited. "You know business has been rough lately, right? I mean, it's been turning around, but I'm behind on my loan payments for the shop."

"Yeah." It would be impossible not to notice, even though she tries to shield me from the money side of things. Mom's spent almost every waking moment keeping that shop going. It makes us money, sort of, but never quite enough to keep our heads above water. I've grown up watching every nickle and dime, even when she didn't ask me to. "Why? Don't tell me you finally have to close?" Mom's world will crumble if that's the case.

"No! The opposite. Someone's invested in us. We're up to date on the payments again. We're in the black, Angela!" She laughs happily, and I can almost picture her dancing around with her phone.

"Seriously? That's awesome! What happened? Who is it? I didn't even know you were looking for investors."

"I wasn't." I can hear the smile in her voice. "And, he's anonymous."

"Anonymous?" It sounds like she knows more than she's letting on.

"Well, he was. Your ol' mom can be a bit of a sleuth when she wants to be." Remembering her finding cigarettes in my drawers when I was fifteen, or finding out that I'd been sneaking sips out of our liquor bottles by measuring the content levels with a ruler when I was sixteen, I believe it. If she suspects something, she's good at uncovering it. She continues happily. "Well, I did some Googling and found out that the company that invested is actually owned by Caldwell Industries."

Whoa. Seriously? Gavin wasn't wrong when he said my mother won the lottery. "You mean Herbert—"

"Of course! Who else could it be? He hasn't said a word, but it came from this little company I'd never heard of. When I looked them up online, the website said they're a subsidiary of Herbie's company. It has to be him. He's so modest. I bet he didn't want me to feel like I owed him something. Now that's true love." Mom's practically bubbling over with excitement.

"God, you're acting like you're fifteen, Mom." I laugh with her. "What's next? You going to tear petals off flowers or carve your initials into the tree in the backyard?"

"Oh, come on. Let your mother have her giddy

moments every once in a while, huh? This is huge. He's saved my business. Now I suddenly have the financial backing to promote and get our name out there. Maybe improve the shop a little. Get better quality inventory. All sorts of things." She gets quiet for a second. "I'm sorry, baby. I know you're hurting. I just had to get that off my chest."

"It's okay. Honest. He ended up being a real jerk." Massive understatement. "I'm really happy for you. You deserve a break." I smile. It's nice to get some good news today. It was rough learning about why Paul ended up black, blue and Violet. I giggle at my own joke, but quietly so I don't have to explain.

"I'm supposed to meet Herbie, so I'm just getting ready. Are you coming home tonight?"

Yeah, probably not. "Nah, I'm going to hang with Cassie a couple of more nights, I think. It's been a while since we've had some just us time, you know? And with college coming up and everything…" I hate lying to Mom, but she'll kill me if she finds out where I really am. I'll probably have to tell her sooner or later, a two week sleepover isn't very believable, but I can stall for a couple of days at least.

"Of course. I understand completely. In fact, that

gives me the perfect opportunity to thank Herbie properly, if you know what I—"

"Stop! There are some things I don't need to know, Mom." I wrinkle my nose at the thought, but I can't help laughing either. It's really funny to hear her acting like a teenager. Puppy love at forty-seven. Who'd have thought?

She laughs too. "Alright, I get it. I'm just excited." She draws a breath, reining in the giggles. "Listen, I'm going to go, but let me know when you know when you're coming home. I want some girl time with my girl too, alright? "

"I know, Mom. Me too. Just, you know… hang a sock on the front door in case I forget to knock. There's only so much trauma I can take."

She laughs. "Will do. Love you, Honey."

"Love you, Mom."

I hang up, thinking about Mom's new love and what that means for me. I'm stuck with Gavin. He might not be such a bad guy underneath it all, but I'm not convinced I can really trust him. Still, just because I don't hate him doesn't mean I can't give him a hard time. That's what little sisters are all about, aren't they? Even if they're stepsisters?

And I can't think of a better place to start than dinner. He won't know what hit him.

16 GAVIN

When Angie walks in, my hors d'oeuvre almost gets stuck in my throat. Wouldn't that be hilarious? Death by a pig in a fucking blanket. A near porked-to-death experience. Goddamn, she looks fantastic. I saw the dress in the store, but all made up? She fucking owns the place.

The bright red fabric waves like a flag, taunting all the bulls in the room. Bet they'd love a go, but she's here for me. She's put her hair up in a naughty librarian bun, pinned in place with some fancy stick thing, and I'm already fantasizing about tugging it out and watching her hair come loose as I push her onto our bed.

Sashaying across the room, putting one foot right

in front of the other as she struts in her new black stilettos, her hips sway in a way that's fucking hypnotic. Hips I want to grab. That I want to hold onto while I have her bent over the bed, while I pound into her. She sees me from across the room, and from her knowing smile, I'm guessing my jaw's currently scraping the floor. I don't give a fuck.

Jesus H. Christ.

I mean, yeah, obviously I know she's fucking hot, but damn. As she gets closer, I see she's put on bright red lipstick that matches the dress. I want that lipstick smeared down my cock. If she doesn't tone it down, I might just pick her up and carry her right up to the room, and she can scream all she wants about chastity vows on the way, because we both know it's not a question of yes or no, only when.

She laughs quietly as she closes in. "You're going to catch flies like that." She's trying to keep cool, but her voice is a little husky. I love it. Still, I close my mouth.

I'm not the only one staring. Almost every eye in the restaurant is on her, and on cruise that's basically packed with the rich and attractive, that's saying something. I should grab her and carry her off before someone she doesn't think is an asshole decides he needs to trade in his trophy wife for a younger model.

But Angie? She hasn't noticed a thing. She's got one of those cherry red lips caught between her teeth, and she only has eyes for me. Waiting for me to say something, like she cares what I think. What I think, is that no matter what I said earlier that day, she's the one with class.

"You look fucking fantastic, babe." I offer my arm to her. "Every single guy in the room is jealous of me right now, knowing it's me and not them who's going to take you up to the room and bang you tonight."

She blinks a couple of times before she takes my arm and laughs. "In your dreams, asshole." Her tone is friendly and happy, but low enough that no one can hear the actual words.

A smile spreads on my face as I take us to our table. Yesterday she would've stormed off after a comment like that, but now she laughs and throws it right back.

The captain stands when we get to the table. He's tall. Taller than me, even, which doesn't happen often. He's older, short hair peppered with grey. He stands like he's got a rod up his ass and I bet he's ex-Navy. His beard's neatly trimmed, not a hair is out of place. He doesn't need his white dress uniform to show he's the captain, but I'm sure the ladies love it.

His whole look seems contrived to look as *handsome sea captain* as possible. He looks me over, probably noting that my clothes say money, but my attitude says 'fuck you'. We're both players, we just use different rules.

Holding out his hand to Angie, he takes hers and bends to kiss it. "Welcome aboard my vessel, Miss Wilson. No wonder Mr. Caldwell's taken to you. If you're as kind as you're beautiful, he's a lucky man indeed. My name is Captain Charles Melbourne."

Smooth moves, Popeye.

Her soft pink blush goes bright red. She does a semblance of a curtsy, but looks completely taken aback by his approach. "Tha—Thank you, Captain Melbourne."

Is she actually falling for this shit?

"Please, call me Chuck." He turns to me and extends his hand. Our handshake's one of those grapples for dominance, both of us squeezing like we're trying to force the other to cry uncle. Neither of us does, but I hope his hand's as sore as mine. His steely gray eyes meet mine and he grins. "Nice to meet you, Mr. Caldwell."

"Please, call me Ga—Herb. Yeah, call me Herb." Oh fucking hell. I should've stuck with Mr. Caldwell. I glance at Angie and she looks like she's barely containing her laughter. Oh, I'm gonna fucking get her for that later.

"Very well, Herb. Thank you. Now if you'd like to be seated, I believe the rest of our guests are here. He gestures. "Mrs. Joyce Merriweather, Mrs. Mabel van der Pelt." Oh, the two oldies from check-in. "Mr. Hank Lennox and his wife Tracy, Mr. David Browning and his wife Melissa, and last, but certainly not least, Mr. Cole Elswood and his very lovely wife Karen."

I greet all of them, knowing I won't remember a single name after five minutes or so. They don't matter anyway. Why should it, when we aren't even who we're supposed to be?

Our seats are right next to the Captain, with Angie on his left, me on her left, then Joyce and so on all the way around the table. A whole evening to play newlyweds. What can possibly go wrong?

Captain Melbourne... Chuck seizes onto Angie almost immediately. Between them making small talk on one side and Joyce busily entertaining Mabel on the other, I'm feeling just a little ignored. Angie is *my* fake fiancée. I don't expect any better from Chuck, but she should at least pretend to give me her full attention. So I do what I do best. Make trouble.

I butt in, shifting my chair closer and putting my arms around her waist. "How's it going, honeybuns?"

She starts at my touch, but keeps her happy girlfriend mask on. "Just peachy, pookie."

"Your wife-to-be's lovely, Herb. What did you do to deserve her?" Chuck laughs, and it sounds really fucking condescending to me. I'm just going to assume he isn't going to actually put the moves on my fiancée, but he's definitely posturing. Even if we're just faking, it still pisses me off.

But I can do fake smiles too. "Oh, I don't know, Chuck. I just treat her the best I can, you know. Give her the world and she'll never need more."

"Oh, of course. I'm sure a woman as beautiful as her gets a lot of attention." He's really talking at her more than me when he says it. Angie looks like she's eating it up, which bugs the hell out of me. Smiling and chewing her lower lip, she's looking at him with huge eyes, looking very impressed. I kick her ankle to get her attention.

She plants the heel of her shoe on my foot and turns towards me. "What is it, dear?"

God, those lips. Her voice is pleasant, but her eyes sparkle with amusement. She's fucking playing me.

Shit, I have nothing to say. That's a first. "Have you tried the scallops? They're really good."

"Oh, Herbie." She pats my cheek softly, laughing when she sees me bristle at the name. "You know I'm allergic to shellfish."

"Right. Of course." I glare at her. "I don't know how I forgot." Maybe because she never told me? This whole conversation is bullshit, but I want her focused on me, and not him.

She turns to the Captain. "You see? He makes me so happy. So eager to share that he forgets himself sometimes. It's like having a little puppy."

They both laugh, and it's at my fucking expense, so I do the mature thing and reach underneath the table and pinch Angie's ass.

"Ow!" She jumps in her chair, then whirls and

glares at me. Serious daggers this time. Poisoned. With teeth.

"Are you alright, Marie?" Chuck asks. She'd given him her mother's name when she sat down, which was good thinking. I have no idea how much information they have on us or not. Angie can be frustrating, but she pays attention.

"What? Yes, sorry. Just a muscle that cramped for a second. It happens sometimes. A serious pain in my backside." She smiles sweetly, and I grin at her little jab.

"Oh, I understand. In fact that reminds me of a story from back in the Navy." For the next fifteen minutes we're subjected to the most self fucking centered saga I've ever heard. Chuck's apparently filled every possible role that exists on the sea, and his tale is basically one long brag about him in a boat with a leak before it sank.

Fine, so it was during a storm and his navigator had spent most of the storm hanging over the rail, puking his guts out. The compass was spinning wildly, the engine only fired half the time and there might have been a fucking kraken or something. I don't know. Pretty sure he's just making shit up. Angie looks fucking enthralled though.

I have no clue whether she really believes him, or if she's doing it just to annoy me, but she's got me pissed either way. I'm just about to pinch her again when someone kicks my shoe. I turn and find Joyce's eyes on me, looking like she thinks she's so damned clever.

I misplace my charm and snap at her, "What?"

She completely ignores my tone. "She's not interested in him, you know."

"Of course not." Am I that obvious? "Why?"

"We had a little chat earlier. She's a sweet girl." Joyce pauses to take a sip of her wine. "You hurt her today. It was obvious."

Wait, Angie's confiding in old ladies now? "So why wouldn't she leave, then?" I'm half amused, half curious.

"If you can make her that mad, she's got a soft spot for you. Only those you love can truly hurt you." She smiles warmly and puts her wrinkled old hand on top of mine. It's like talking relationships with my grandmother, except mine is probably on a beach in Cabo with her new boy toy. Come to think of it, they'd probably get along great.

I return her smile. "Good to know." I shrug. "I just have to do my best to make it up to her." My teeth ache from all this sweet talk. We're engaged and I'm supposed to be in love and shit, when I really only want to turn around and bust Chuck's Pinocchio nose.

Joyce narrows her eyes at me. "Are you good with your tongue?"

"What?" She didn't just ask what I think she did, did she?

"You want to make it up to her. Don't you? A good tongue will get you far. Henry... he was my favorite husband, you see. Number three. Anyway, Henry could do this little thing with his tongue that drove me crazy. Right up the wall." Her gaze goes distant while she remembers.

I laugh quietly. Yeah, she and Grandma would get along just fine. They're both fucking nuts. But whatever. She seems nice enough.

She snaps back to the present. "Anyway, all I'm saying is this, young man, a tongue can get you out of as much trouble as it gets you into. It certainly worked on me. Of course that was back when I could get my knees behind my ears. Henry and I were married almost thirty years before his heart attack. Oh, I miss him still."

I try not to shudder visibly. I mean, sure I know old people have sex. I bet it's fucking great. Awesome. Beyond belief. I hope I'm one of them someday. I could live without the visual though.

"Just think about it, dearie." She winks, then returns her attention to her friend, leaving me confused and a little bit queasy. I shake my head and turn back to Angie and Chuck.

"So there I was, and I swear the shark I had on my hook was thirty feet long. At least. The biggest shark I've seen before or since. Massive. It fought like it knew it was facing the end of its days, pulling and charging and doing everything it could to drag me into the water rather than the other way around. Hell, I had six guys lined up to keep me on board, one after the other. We didn't have a proper shark-fishing chair, and so we just jammed ourselves up against the railing and prayed we'd pull the beast up over the rail." Chuck wipes his face like he's getting sweaty just telling the most ridiculous fishing tale ever.

"Anyway, as I mentioned before, we were going through the Gulf of Aden at the time, which is a hotbed of piracy any time of year. On top of that, it was a particularly rough year for unrest in Somalia, so there we were, right in the middle of hauling aboard the largest shark possibly recorded ever, anywhere, and all of us unable to take our eyes off the gruesome battle of life and death unfolding in our wake.

"But something, a feeling or a kind of premonition, spooked me. I looked up for a second, and spotted them. The pirates were almost on top of us, gaining quickly in six powerful speed boats. They were already so close I could read the ruthless expressions on their faces and see that they were armed to the teeth. Their decks were so loaded down with firepower, I was surprised they didn't sink, much less be able to come at us so quickly.

"So I was faced with a tough decision: defeat the king of all sharks, or save my crew. Reluctantly, I released my fishing pole and let the shark drag it into the inky depths. Then we scrambled to our stations to escape."

Is this guy for fucking real? Not sure what amazes me more. That he's able to spout off all this horseshit with a straight face, or that Angie's watching him with wide eyes and her sexy little mouth half open.

"How did you get away?" Angie's playing right into his hands. I give her a quick kick under the table, but she ignores me. Really? I'll stream Jaws for her if she wants a crazy shark story. It's probably just as real.

Chuck's only happy to keep on spewing crap. "This is where the story gets really incredible. It looked bad. Real bad. Our ship wasn't quick enough to get away, and at the rate the pirates were coming, we realized running was impossible. We were just getting out harpoon guns, flare pistols and anything else we could conceivably use for a weapon, when something happened that I've never seen the likes of and probably never will again.

"The closest boat was just about to come into boarding range, when the water exploded underneath it. Surging out of the ocean like a watery demon hell-bent on revenge, the same goddamn shark we'd been fighting for the last hour surfaced with the boat in its very jaws! I'm not joking when I say it almost capsized us, and launched them a full twenty feet into the air. When it struck the water, their boat broke clear in two.

"The other boats stopped, their crews yelling in panic. Like the demons they are, they left their buddies to their watery deaths, turned and raced off as fast as their overpowered engines would take them. Even then, they weren't quite fast enough. The shark nailed another one, capsizing it and spilling everyone onboard into the water. It was the craziest damn sight I've seen in my whole life, but without that shark, I might not be sitting here today, and that's the truth."

"Oh Chuck, that's amazing. You must've been terrified." When I see her put her hands on his jacket sleeve, that's enough. Maybe she thinks I'm an ass, but I'm not going to sit here while she fawns over a bullshitter like him, just because he's got more stripes on his sleeve than I do.

So I pinch her ass again.

"Yow!" She turns to me and hisses in a sharp whisper. "What the hell is your problem?"

Putting my hand on her thigh, I grip it tightly, whispering back. "My problem is that you're a piss-poor fiancée. If we're going to pull this off, we can't let them figure out that we're not our parents."

She gives me a look like she thinks I'm an idiot. "What, are the cruise line ninjas hiding under our table or something? Why on earth would they even suspect anything?" She frowns. "At least Chuck's entertaining, which is more than I can say for you. You can sit and brood all you want, but I'm at the Captain's table, and I'm going to enjoy it." And with that she turns back to him.

Fuck that. "Babe." I pinch her ass again. When she turns this time, I'm ready, sliding one hand to her waist and the other behind her head, forcing her to lean towards me. Meeting her between our chairs, I cover her lips with mine. Fuck, she tastes good.

She struggles, but only for a second. I want to think that it's my amazing kiss, but she's probably just remembered who we're supposed to be. Gripping her tightly, I claim her mouth. It's mine, like the rest of her, even if she doesn't know it yet.

But then it's like a dam breaks. Her hands come around me, and instead of just putting up with my kiss, she meets it, melting into my arms. Our tongues dance while I forget the whole fucking room, the Captain, everything. Her eyes close, but I can't keep my gaze off her beautiful face. Sliding my hand up along her side, tracing her delicious curves, I want to tear that dress off right here and now and I don't fucking care how much it cost.

When we finally part, both of us breathing hard, her whole face is flushed and her eyes intent on mine. It's the kind of look I want to see beneath me, a look that says, "Fuck me again." My cock strains against my pants, so I hope we're getting dessert. I'm going to need a little time before standing.

She chews her lower lip and our eyes remain locked for several long seconds. The spell's broken when I hear an excited little clap behind me. It's Joyce, staring at us with the most gleeful expression that borders on crazy. "You kids are so adorable! What did I tell you, right? Tongues."

Angie pulls away from me, looking embarrassed, but... pleased? She turns back to the captain with a mysterious smile on her lips. Soon she's back to listening to his tall tales, but this time it doesn't bother me so much. This dinner needs to end, though. Soon.

The waiters clear off the table, and I've barely eaten a bite. I don't get why I let him get under my skin like that. It's not like Captain Chuck over there's going to steal her away from me. That look Angie gave me after our kiss? I want it all the time. We're faking a lot on this cruise, but that was real.

Dessert's served, and it's crème brûlée. I grimace. The lowest common denominator of fancy desserts. My stomach rumbles, though, so I dig in like it's food. I'll get room service later.

"So Herb…" Chuck doesn't even register until Angie kicks my shin. Fuck, her shoes are sharp. Also, gotta remember that I'm Herb. "Are you ready for tomorrow's big event, then?" He winks at me, while Angie and I exchange confused glances.

"Absolutely." I have no fucking idea. "Ready as ever. You going to be there?"

He laughs, a real belly laugh while he points at me. I chuckle along, but seriously, I really should figure out what this is all about. First the guy at my door this morning, now this. What did Dad have planned for Marie? I'm starting to think we're in for a serious surprise tomorrow, and it won't be good.

17 ANGIE

Sun streams in through the window, searing my eyelids and forcing me awake. Blinking and rubbing my eyes, I shake my head to clear the cobwebs. Right. The cabin. The ship. Gavin. This morning there's no warm, solid body behind me. He's not here. Seems I have the room to myself.

It's stupid to be disappointed, and probably just as well. Yesterday was crazy. Shopping, our fight, finding out about Paul, the dinner… The Captain was hilarious, and the food had been so good. Everything had been so fancy, and I'd fit right in. Even Gavin had been good, mostly.

And then there was the kiss.

My breath speeds up just at the thought, and I

hate myself for how easily Gavin can do that to me. Life was simpler when could pretend it was just his body I liked. Is that idiot actually getting to me? Throwing myself back on the bed with a groan, I breathe out heavily, trying to think.

I was supposed to be on this cruise to have fun, with Paul. He was going to be my first. It would be perfect and we'd enjoy good food and complimentary champagne while we spent a couple of weeks together. Instead I'm stuck here with *him*.

When did the good guy turn into the bad guy, and the bad guy into the… not as bad guy?

I'd held out a little hope that Paul would call me back and explain, but he hasn't, and I'm actually a little relieved. So many warning signs I'd ignored are obvious in hindsight. Better to find out before we slept together, but it still sucks. So now I'm single again, but it's not like I can do anything about it here. Everyone thinks Gavin and I are getting married.

The bathroom door opens with a loud click, scaring the crap out of me. Gavin sticks his head out, hair dripping and broad, muscular torso exposed. He keeps his lower half covered behind the wall, making me wonder if he's naked or not. Memories of his hard ass, his powerful legs, and his big cock spraying cum all over the shower door flash through my mind.

At this rate I'm going to need the shower. Cold.

He glances around the room before his eyes settle on me in just my underwear. He smiles slyly before speaking. "You alright? I thought I heard a noise."

I roll my eyes at him. "Yeah, I'm fine."

"Ah, alright." He makes as if to close the door, but opens it again. "You weren't playing with yourself, were you?"

"Get real!" Doesn't he think of anything else? *Speak for yourself, Angie.* "No!"

"Were you thinking of me?" He leans forward, exposing just a little bit more. He's got a bit of a trail of hair down the middle of his stomach and it leads straight to...

I have to think of something else. "You're a perv."

He laughs and shuts the door, leaving me to imagine him in the shower, all naked and dripping, the water running down those hard pecs and dripping off his muscular ass and... Oh, quit it! I wasn't playing with myself, but now that my mind's heading in that direction, it's tempting to slip back in under the covers and slide a hand right into my panties.

I don't, but more out of principle than anything else. Like I'd be letting him win. Well, that and I have no idea how much longer he's going to be in there. I glance at the clock. 10:52. Outside, the weather's beautiful, so maybe I'll grab my bathing suit and catch some sun. Maybe some margaritas if I'm lucky. They don't seem to bother carding me onboard, probably because of our reservations.

I change quickly before Gavin comes back out, and I'm just about to open the door when there's a knock on the other side. Opening up, I find another pimple faced steward with a fuzzy attempt of a moustache perched on his upper lip. I doubt he's even eighteen. Who hires these guys?

"I—I'm sorry, Miss Wilson. Just the wake-up call you ordered." He seems nervous, but that doesn't keep his eyes from roaming over my body. I should've grabbed my wrap before I opened the door. He's got to see girls in bathing suits every day, though. Bet that makes work awkward.

"Wake-up call? What for?" I can't imagine Gavin called for anything like that, and I definitely didn't.

His eyes never quite make it back up past my chest. "Um… I can't really say, Miss Wilson. I'm not allowed to." He swallows, looking uncomfortable.

"Wait, you're here to wake me up, but you can't say why?" This is ridiculous.

"It's per Mr. Caldwell's orders, Miss Wilson." Shifting from foot to foot, he looks ready to run away. "I—I think it's a surprise."

"What kind of surprise?" I frown, but he doesn't see it. "Hey, eyes up here."

Realizing he's been caught, he quickly straightens and looks at me. Well, a bit off to the side, avoiding meeting my eyes, but closer than before. His face has turned bright red. "I'm sorry. I can't. I have clear instructions from my boss."

With a sigh, I let him off the hook. "Alright. Thanks. I'll let him know."

"Thank you, Miss Wilson." He takes off at an almost run.

Gavin's still in the shower. I'll tell him about the mysterious arrangements later. Maybe. Or maybe I'll just enjoy my day in the sun and hope he doesn't find me. I grab my wrap, a towel and my e-reader, then slide my key card into my bikini top and slam the door shut behind me.

Skipping the elevator, I follow the winding stairs down instead. It feels good to move a little. My flip flops echo off the metal walls. After God knows how many turns, I see a door labeled UPPER FRONT DECK. It's heavy, but I get it open and step out into the sunlight.

Wow. The deck is in full activity. If it's not every crew member on the ship, it's got to be close. They're all busy setting up tables and hanging decorations. Is there something going on later? Party streamers and brightly colored balloons hang between the white parasols that hover over tables and sun chairs. Someone having a birthday maybe?

"Miss Wilson. Marie. What are you doing out here?" Captain Chuck separates from the crowd, crossing over the deck towards me with long determined strides. He's wearing his dress whites again. Maybe every day is dress-up day for him. "You're not supposed to be out here yet. Didn't Herb tell you?"

"Tell me what?" There's a conspiracy going on, and eventually *someone's* going to tell me what's going on, right?

"Oh no, you're not getting me to ruin it." He smiles broadly. His voice turns formal, though his grin doesn't fade. "I'm sorry, Miss, but I'm going to have to ask you to keep off this deck until further notice. If you'd like to sunbathe, feel free to use the lower sun deck, or the aft deck, but I'm afraid the upper front deck is off limits until 6:00 PM." He leans in conspiratorially and winks. "Then of course, your attendance is mandatory."

Mandatory, huh? Another dinner probably. I wonder what Herbert had arranged for Mom. She's a lucky woman. "Fine." I hold up my hands in defeat. "I'll go to the aft deck. This had better be good, Captain Chuck."

He laughs. "Oh, it will be." Then he shoos me off.

I suppose I'll have to wait, but at least I know when and where now.

18 ANGIE

The aft deck is a couple of levels down. First things first. My stomach's growling, and I see a snack bar. Or deck bistro, as they call it. Taking one of the stools, I watch the ocean stream by us while I eat one of the most delicious burgers I've had in my life, and everything just goes on the room tab. That's luxury right there. Not a bad life if you can get it, or marry it I suppose.

Burger devoured, I go further aft to where the chairs are. Picking one in the sun at random, I sit and lose myself in a sci fi romance. Wacky and totally unbelievable, but I love the characters. I move around a bit, in and out of the sun so I don't fry, but amazingly enough, a couple of hours go by without anything horrible happening. No Paul, no Gavin, no drama. *This* I could get used to.

When I think I've pushed my tanning about as far as it can go, I switch to a chair that looks like it'll be in the shade for a while, and in the process find my favorite couple of retired cruise enthusiasts dozing next to me. Joyce and Mabel are in light summer shirts and slacks, all white. They have the cruise wardrobe down pat. Almost enough to make a girl feel underdressed.

I give them a smile and pull my chair closer. Almost immediately one of the servers comes by with a choice of cool drinks. I grab an iced tea and set it on the metal table next to my chair.

"Miss Wilson." Joyce is looking straight at me.

"Please, call me Ang—Marie. Call me Marie." Crap. I almost forget my cover. This pretending stuff drives me nuts. One thing was fooling the concierge, but I feel bad giving a fake name to everyone. I bet Joyce wouldn't even care, but I don't want to chance it.

If she notices my slip-up, she doesn't show it. "Of course, dearie. Thank you." She tilts her chair up with a bit of effort, leaning forward to talk. "I remember when I was young and beautiful like you." She might be a bit nutty, but she's sweet.

"Thank you. You're still so beautiful now, I'm sure you were a knockout then." It's true, she has one of those faces where you can almost see the beautiful young woman under the surface.

Joyce laughs. "You forgot to add 'for my age' to that, Marie. But, I appreciate it." She looks off in the distance, like she's remembering something. "When I was young, I had all the boys falling at my feet. Enjoy it while you can. Life is so short and fleeting." For a moment, she sounds wistful, but then she speaks with renewed energy. "But those are old people worries, and you're far too young for those. So, tell me, Marie, are you excited?"

"Excited?" I have my suspicions that this is tied to whatever's happening on the upper deck. Does everyone on this ship know what it's about except us?

"Oh, so he really hasn't told you yet, has he?" Her smile is mischievous, and she looks ready to burst with it.

I decide to pump her for some info. All this secrecy is getting pretty irritating. "So…" I drag it out while I eye her with a conspiratorial grin. "What's going to happen? You can tell me, can't you?"

"Oh no, young lady. If your husband-to-be hasn't seen fit to tell you, I'm not going to spill the beans. I don't want that brute coming after me if he finds out I ruined his fun." Joyce laughs, eyes bright and obviously not terribly worried about Gavin.

I roll my eyes, but I can't really get mad at her. "What do you think he's going to do? Give you a spanking?" Images of yesterday morning flash before my eyes, and I feel a tingle that runs right down to my core.

This time she laughs outright. "Maybe?" She adds eagerly, "Is he good at it?" My iced tea catches in my throat, unleashing a wave of rolling coughs while I try to get my breath back. "Oh dear. Should I hit your back?" She makes as if to get up.

Waving my hand at her and shaking my head, I make her sit back down. "I'm—" Another cough. "I'm alright. Just went down the wrong way." I get my breathing back under control. "What were you asking again?" Then I remembered.

"Well, I don't think I have to tell you that you've picked a tough one, do I? Handsome of course, but he looks like a spanker, that one." She winks with a mischievous grin. "Like my first husband, Jim. He was a strong believer in discipline. And with those big hands of his…" She trails off, lost in the memories, while I stare at her in disbelief. "Well, let me tell you, some days I was too sore to sit." She sighs, like she's remembering fond times. "Those were the best days."

I hide my stunned expression behind sipping my drink. "That's very… interesting. What happened to Jim?"

"He was run over by the town drunk many years ago. It was a shock, but at least it was quick. He never knew what hit him, poor man." She sighs.

"I'm so sorry," I say, horrified. Some days I just can't keep my foot out of my mouth.

"Oh, it's alright, dear. It was many, many years ago. He was a good man. Strict and firm, but a good man. And boy, did he know how to tan an ass." She grins broadly at what apparently are some very good memories for her, disturbing as that seems.

"He sounds like he was…" I was a bit at a loss for words. "An interesting man to live with."

She titters. "That he was. He was my first, you know? First everything. I was only seventeen when we married, but we were together for over twenty years before his accident. He put four children in me, boom, boom, boom, right in a row. Virile as a bull."

I want to say it's all the sun that's making my face all red, but it wouldn't be the truth. She certainly doesn't hold back.

"Hang on to your first one, Marie. They're always special. Just you wait and see." There's a certainty in her voice that makes me wonder. "Anyway…" She braces against her deck chair and stands. "I should get Mabel upstairs so we can get ready. It takes a while when you get to be our age, and she needs a little extra help."

Nodding, I get up to offer a hand. Together, we get Mabel on her feet, then Joyce leads her towards the elevators. Mabel mentions something about a lunch buffet, which makes Joyce smile. "Yes, Mabel. Soon. But first we're getting ready."

Shaking my head with a grin, I watch them until they're out of sight. She's something else. I return to my chair and read for a while before I feel my eyelids get heavy. Putting my book down, I roll over and shift my chair to be flat. I cross my arms so I can rest my head on them and it's not long before I doze off in the shade.

19 ANGIE

I wake up to strong hands rubbing my back. Hard, powerful hands, firmly massaging lotion into my skin. I close my eyes, enjoying the sensation, his touch hot even under the sun bearing down on us. God, that feels good.

My eyes shoot open. Wait a minute. Who the hell is it? I roll off the deck chair with a yelp, landing in an awkward crouch and looking up. Gavin. I should've guessed.

He's got his hands out in a "Who? Me?" gesture, mouth turned up in that infuriating smirk that drives me nuts. "What? You were starting to burn. Just a little sunblock."

The sun's moved while I was sleeping. I probably

would have turned into a tomato, but still... "You could've asked first."

"How do you know I didn't? You were asleep."

"You can't just start rubbing people in their sleep!"

"Pretty sure I just did."

"You know what I mean!" So much for peace and quiet.

He shrugs. "Fine. As you wish." He bends and picks something up from the deck chair. Something white, which he balls up and carries with him. "You have fantastic tits, by the way."

My mouth drops open as I realize he's holding my top. Oh shit. He must've untied it while he was putting on the lotion. I was so mad I didn't notice, and now he's taking off with it. "Come back with that!" Clutching an arm across my chest, I chase after him.

He laughs out loud and takes off, running just fast enough to keep ahead of me. "I'm sorry, are you missing something?" he calls out over his shoulder.

"Stop being an ass, Gavin." I stop, scowling at his back. He turns around and waves my top in the air. There's no point in chasing him. I refuse to stoop to his level and play that game. "You've had your fun. Come on, give it here before someone sees me."

He shakes it teasingly. "Giving up already?"

"Oh, cut it out. Hand it over." I glance around to see if anyone's watching, but this part of the deck is deserted except for us. At least there's that.

As I stalk forwards with one arm covering my breasts, he stays put, lifting his arm to keep my top just barely out of reach. "I want to see you jump for it." He grins broadly, his cheeks dimpling. How did I never notice those dimples before?

I glare at him, up at the annoying slip of white cloth and then back at him. There's no way I'm giving him the satisfaction of watching me bounce around topless. I need a different plan. Work smarter, not harder.

Stepping right up close, I put my free hand softly onto his tight abs, tracing each ridge with my fingertips as I slide upwards to his chest. My breath catches, and I have to remember why I'm doing this. I'm trying to distract him, but that's not going to help if I can't focus. "You know, maybe you're right."

He looks down at me, not lowering the top an inch. "I know I'm right. What about?" His eyes sparkle with mischief. The game's still on his terms.

I walk my fingers across his right pec, stopping to swirl my index finger lazily around his nipple. It hardens up immediately, and I get the urge to lick it. To swirl my tongue around it instead of my finger. *Angie, stay on target.* "Maybe the two of us... you know..."

He laughs, his chest shaking under my touch. "No. I don't know. Why don't you tell me, babe?" His voice is teasing, confident. Out of the corner of my eye, I see his arm has come down just a touch.

Sliding my hand up onto his shoulder, I marvel at the powerful muscles underneath. I trace their contours before I continue down his upper arm, following a dark spiral of ink. "I mean, I know you're going to be my stepbrother and all, but..." I trail off, dragging it out.

"But what, babe?" He's leaning in just a little, his head coming closer and the arm holding my top lowering.

I go for broke. Pressing my naked torso against his and my cheek against his broad chest, it's hard to pretend that I'm only doing this to distract him anymore. His nipples aren't the only ones that are hard, and mine are tight and sensitive as they drag along his stomach. Still, I've got my head angled so I can keep an eye on the prize. I just hope he lowers it enough that I can snag it before I throw all my principles overboard and jump him.

I'm not sure if mashing my breasts against him is any better than giving him a quick show, but it definitely feels better to me. I have both hands on him now, playing over his hot skin, down his sides and onto his hips. God, he feels so good against me. I don't have to pretend to be short of breath. "But maybe, I mean if you don't think it's wrong…"

So close now. He looms over me, and I think he's going to kiss me, but he's moving slowly. "It's alright, babe, you can tell me." Chuckling softly, he puts his free arm at the small of my back, rubbing my skin just above the top of my bikini bottom and holding me in place.

I can't help it. I nuzzle against his chest, hearing his slow, steady heartbeat. It's not his arm keeping me trapped. I'm doing a fine job of that myself. Looking for my top, I spot it just within reach. Am I quick enough? I'll have to be. Otherwise I don't think I'll be able to pull away. I put a soft kiss right by his nipple, taking a bit of satisfaction in hearing him draw a sharp breath. I'm getting to him, at least a little. Preparing to leap, I whisper soft words, too quietly for him to hear.

"I can't hear you, babe." He leans in so close that I hear his deep voice right in my ear, sending shivers ratcheting down my spine.

"I said..." My whisper trails off, and I go for it. "That you're an asshole!" I catch him completely off guard, my left hand snagging my top right out of his fingers while my right swings up and leaves a bright red mark on his cheek with a smack, all done in a fancy twirl that puts me facing away from him so he doesn't get more of a show than necessary. I've never put my top on so quickly before.

Behind me, Gavin laughs. "That was so totally worth it. You want me, babe."

"Fuck you."

Suddenly he's behind me, his arms around me and his chest pressing against my back. His voice is a husky whisper right in my ear, "I'd love to." Something nudges the small of my back. Oh my God, he's hard.

I tear away from him and spin. The lump in his

board shorts is huge, and I miss the feel of it pressing against me. "Not in a million years. No way. Never. Not if my life depended on it."

His face takes on a mock hurt expression. "Really, Angie? Your very life? I can't be *that* fucking bad." Cocking his arm, he flexes. "I know you like my body, at least. That's what you wanted the first time we met. You know, when you were just looking for a quick... hard... messy..." Each word brings him a step closer, and each word raises more goosebumps. "...fuck." He nods. "You would've gotten it, too. Remember that. But I guess now you're too *principled.*"

"It's good one of us is. Just leave me alone, Gavin." He's an ass. So why does he make my heart pound and my panties so damn wet?

"You know what? I would, but I had a real reason for coming down before we started playing." He shrugs. "That thing that they keep reminding us about starts now. We're running a little late, actually."

Really, it's almost six already? I look around, finding the sun getting low on the horizon. Amazing how time flies when you don't have anything you have to do.

I roll my eyes at him, thinking of a million things I'd rather do than attend some function with him. "Can't we skip it? Or you go, and tell them I have a headache or something."

Gavin shakes his head. "I think we better show. The way they've been going on about it, Dad must've set it up, and it'd be pretty fucking weird if we weren't there." He shrugs again. "It's probably something for you."

That would only make me feel better if I knew what it was. With a sigh, I make sure my suit's properly back on, then nod. "Fine. This'd better be good, though."

He leads the way. Up two flights and we're back at the heavy door labeled UPPER FRONT DECK. When Gavin opens it effortlessly, I glare at him, but at least he holds it for me.

I step through to a deck covered with decorations. I'd seen the balloons earlier, but now there are flowers everywhere, mostly white, but beautifully accented with bright colors. Soft classical music plays from the speakers, setting a solemn mood.

And the people! The deck is packed with what

seems like just about every passenger on the whole ship. What are they all doing here? As soon as we stepped through the door, all conversation stopped, and now they're all staring at us. I glance at Gavin, but he only shrugs.

A red carpet runner starts at our feet and parts the crowd right down the middle towards the front of the deck. I follow it with my eyes to where it ends at an arch covered in vines and flowers. Standing next to it, still in full dress whites, is Captain Chuck, looking smug and distinguished at the same time.

I swallow. That's an altar. Those are guests. The captain's officiating. I start to hyperventilate. I glance back at Gavin and I see from his dropped jaw and wide eyes that he's realized what I just did.

"Oh shit," we whisper in chorus.

20 GAVIN

Holy fuck.

Seriously.

Holy.

Fuck.

Dad doesn't fuck around, but I can't fucking believe he was actually planning on fucking marrying Marie on the fucking cruise ship.

Fuck.

Now what?

Angie looks like she just had a heart attack. I don't blame her. Pretty sure mine skipped a beat or two just now. It's still racing like I've run a ten-mile. Giving her a nudge with my elbow, I turn on a smile. It's fake as hell, but nobody cares so long as the mask is in place. I figured that out long ago.

She glances at me anxiously, her eyes flitting around like a wild animal ready to make its escape. I hold out my hand and she takes it hesitantly, swallowing the biggest lump in history. "Gavin!" she whispers with a hiss. "It's a wedding. A wedding. For us!"

I step closer to her so we can hear each other more easily, whispering out of the corner of my mouth. "It's for our parents. It won't count."

"We *are* our parents. At least as far as they're concerned. We're not actually going to do this, are we?" There's panic in her whisper, and for a little thing, she has a painful grip when she's freaked out.

"It won't count." I think. "We just have to fake our way through the ceremony, and then we'll have a huge meal and it's business as usual." I squeeze her hand back, trying to comfort her and hoping she doesn't feel how I'm shaking. Fuck, this is some crazy shit.

A steward rushes over to take her things, and we start to walk, still wearing just our swimsuits, and not knowing what else to do. The guests applaud as we walk by them, grinning like fucking idiots. It's the longest walk of my life.

"Are you sure?" Another hiss from Angie. "I mean, what if it *does* count. What do we do?" She's wearing a smile as fake as mine now, but in her eyes is pure panic.

"It won't count. No fucking way. How could it?" Now if only I felt as confident as I'm trying to sound. How does this work? There need to be witnesses and shit, right? Signatures that have to match? Something? Not having any immediate plans of getting married, it's not something I've looked into.

I put an arm around Angie, trying to calm her while I smile and nod to the guests. She's stiff as a pole, shivering, and there's not a thing I can do about it. Well, I did want us to spend more time together. Just like Dad to pull a crazy-ass stunt like this.

Fuck you, Dad.

We stop in front of the arch and Captain Chuck takes a step forward. He straightens, and after giving us what I'm sure is supposed to be a reassuring smile, he speaks in a loud voice. "Welcome, everyone. I'm so glad you're all here to witness this joyful union today." He looks up at the sky. "And boy did we get some beautiful weather for it, didn't we? It's a good thing too, because from the look of them, Herb really went all out keeping it a surprise."

There's amused laughter from the crowd and some scattered applause. Angie looks ready to sink through the deck in embarrassment, but he continues like it's nothing. "Today, I have the pleasure of joining the beautiful Miss Marie Wilson with the love of her life, the handsome Mr. Herbert Caldwell."

Angie's hand crushes my fingers. Her whisper is barely audible. "I'm going to faint."

"You're going to be fine. Just remember, good food and an open bar, right?" I squeeze her hand back. "We're going to get through this, and then we're going to get so shitfaced that we're going to have crawl back to our room. Clear?" She nods nervously. For once we seem to be on the same side. It's a small victory, won under duress, but I'll take it.

"It's not often I get to officiate weddings aboard, so this is as exciting for me as it is for the couple, I bet." Our captain laughs, and the crowd chuckles along.

Laugh it up, Chuck. You have no fucking idea.

He continues, and I hope it won't be for too long. I think the only reason Angie's still standing is because her knees are locked. "Did you all know that captains don't actually have the authority to officiate marriages? It's a myth, but a so pervasive one that the Navy even has a statute dictating that Naval captains are not allowed to do it."

I let out a sigh of relief. "I think we're off the hook. Guess it's just for show." Angie nods in response, looking a little less panicked. Fuck, if it's just for fun, we might as well enjoy it. I pull her closer and place an excited kiss on the top of her head. I half expect her to slap me again, but relief's a powerful thing. Instead, she puts on a cute little smile. I could get used to that.

"Luckily, I'm retired, and I'm not one to let something silly like statutes stop me anyway. So, in the state of Florida I am a registered public notary. Just in case anyone's wondering if this is for real, when we're done, the happy couple will be Mr. and Mrs. Caldwell." Captain Chuck bows to a smattering of applause.

Fuck.

Angie sags in my arms. Shit, did she faint? I grip hard, supporting her, and whisper to her as loud as I dare. "Angie!"

She steadies, then looks at me. Her eyes shimmer, like she's about to cry. "We're getting married."

I laugh it off. "Relax, babe. It'll never stick. We'll pretend to be married, eat and drink 'till we puke and get it annulled when we're back on land if we have to. It'll be fun." She's not convinced, but they can't seriously hold us to this. This isn't real. Me? I'm already looking forward to the champagne and cigars.

21 ANGIE

Shouldn't it take longer to get married? One moment, Gavin and I were standing there in shock, then a short speech, a few words and suddenly we're at the vows.

"I do." My voice is shaky and I barely get the words out. Gavin's "I do" is more confident, and he's grinning like an idiot. What if we're really freaking married? Doesn't he get that this is serious?

Married!

Apparently not, from the confident way he takes my hand and turns us to face the crowd. My face burns while they applaud. This is all fake. This is crazy. Ridiculous. But sometimes it's like you're stuck in a snowball barreling down a mountain, and everything spins faster and faster until you crash into a million pieces against the bottom.

That's this trip.

I just got married to my stepbrother. In a freaking bikini. Crash.

The crowd gets up for a standing ovation. I want to shrink away, but instead I stand here with the biggest fake smile ever on my face, doing my best to look radiant or whatever it is brides are supposed to look like. In flip-flops.

My face is burning with embarrassment, and I'm sure I'm blushing all the way down. They could at least have given me time to put on a dress or a shawl or something. Why did I let the steward take my wrap?

Chuck's voice cuts in behind us. "You may kiss the bride."

Gavin laughs. "I've been waiting for this moment." Wrapping his arms around me, he dips me deeply like I don't weigh a thing, and plants his lips right on mine.

I forget about everything around me, about being married, about being nearly naked, about my embarrassment. About everything. Suddenly, it's just

Gavin and me.

Heat surges through us, connecting us in the moment. His bare skin burns where it touches mine. My blood roars in my ears, rushing hotly through me like an overflowing river and I barely hear the loud cheering of the crowd above it. Hooking my arms around his neck, I grip him by the hair and cling to him like a life preserver.

I'm too wound up. That must be it. My body's on emotional overload right now, and it's discharging in the kiss. Sense creeps slowly back into my mind, making me realize that I'm clinging like a lovesick bride to her brand new husband. Not for show, but because in that moment, he was the most real and sane thing in an ocean of insanity.

The cheering doesn't stop until he pulls back, letting us both come up for air. His eyes crinkle in cocky amusement. "Man, if I knew all it would take was marrying you, I would've done it long ago."

"Fuck you." I say it in my sweetest tone and with a smile on my face.

His smile turns into a predatory grin and his eyes narrow. "Oh, you will. And I can't fucking wait, babe." He swings me back up to my feet, then continues loud enough for everyone to hear. "But first, we party!" Another cheer sounds from the crowd.

Captain Chuck appears behind us and puts a broad hand on each of our backs, guiding us towards a long table set up on the deck. His hand is rough and calloused, but that's it. So why does Gavin's touch make me feel all tingly and warm when I can't even stand him?

I try not to think about it too much as servers show us our seats at the head of the table. The guy who took my stuff comes back, and I slip my wrap on like a makeshift dress. A little too late after he left me to get married in my swimsuit, but at least now I don't feel as exposed, and the air's getting cooler. Gavin sits down in just his board shorts, apparently happy enough with that. Strangest reception ever.

The Captain is seated to my left, and then Joyce and Mabel have places at Gavin's right.

"I knew you folks had spoken before, so I figured you wanted some familiar faces at the table," Chuck grinned.

Joyce is bubbling over with excitement, clapping her hands and talking to Mabel, who seems to be looking for the buffet. One of the stewards directs her back to her chair twice before the servers come with appetizers. It's some kind of sashimi with a delicious dipping sauce, which is melt-in-your-mouth good. I can't believe I'm even thinking it, but maybe Gavin's right. Just enjoy the party, and we'll get everything sorted out when we get home.

A platoon of servers step up, popping champagne bottles at the same time like a twenty-one gun salute. A cheer goes up and flutes are poured. As soon as our glasses are filled, Captain Chuck stands and proclaims a toast to the happy couple. Then someone else does. Then Gavin stands and makes a toast to all the guests, and so on and so on. By the first main course, some kind of fish and crab dish with scallops in an amazing clear sauce, I'm feeling pretty happy, already well into my third glass.

Gavin looks at me curiously when I pop one of the scallops in my mouth and chew it happily. "Babe, didn't you say you were allergic to shellfish?"

"Yup." I giggle, and it's not just the champagne. "I might've said those words."

His eyes widen for a moment, then he laughs. "I'll get you for that." The hot promise in his voice makes my breath catch.

Joyce looks at me with a sparkle in her eye and picks up her dessert spoon. Oh no. Gavin spots her and his face breaks into a large grin. When she starts ringing her glass, he's already leaning in for the kiss. I must be drunk, because I turn to meet him without having to convince myself.

God, he kisses so well. The heat from his lips surges through me, filling my body from the tips of my fingers and down to my toes, but most of it pools right between my legs. When we part I'm breathing heavy, and so is he. Something tells me he's not going to be as easy to push away tonight, and maybe it's the champagne, but right now that doesn't sound so bad.

Joyce was the first to ring her glass, but she definitely isn't the last. Each new kiss is a little bit deeper than the last, and Gavin's letting his hands roam more freely as night falls and it's easier to hide. When he cups my ass and I don't immediately slap him, we're both a bit surprised, I think.

By the time we get to dessert, which is a tall spindly thing that I have no idea what is other than that it tastes deliciously sweet and is decorated with heavenly melted chocolate, my nipples are rubbing against my top, and I'm squirming in my seat. If only I could keep Gavin using his mouth for kissing instead of talking, I might not even want the annulment.

Out on deck, a large area has been set off as a dance floor, and as the servers clear away the last of our dishes, a live band starts up. Chuck's right there with them, picking up the microphone and declaring that it's time for our first dance as a married couple. It's a good thing I'm pretty drunk, because all of my dancing experience comes from dance clubs. Sober, I'd never dare to let Gavin pull me out of my chair and onto the dance floor.

"Just follow my lead, babe." He takes my left hand in his right, puts his left hand at the small of my back, then leads me elegantly around the dance floor while I follow the best I can. He moves confidently, like he's done this a million times, his strong arms nearly carrying me. "Dad insisted I learn this shit growing up. Never thought it'd actually come in handy."

Gavin laughs while doing his best to make me look graceful. It's like I'm floating when I'm in his arms, my head swimming and it's not *just* from the alcohol. Twinkling stars spin above as he twirls me, the wrap floating around my thighs, and when he pulls me back in, I melt into him. I think I'm pretending, but honestly I can't even tell anymore.

The first number ends, and after a round of applause that he receives gracefully and I receive by burying my face against his chest to hide my blush, the other partiers join in.

I try to head back to the table, but Gavin stops me with a tight grip on my arm. He shakes his head, a playful pout on his full lips. "Tell me you are *not* leaving me on the dance floor after only one dance. On our wedding night, no less."

"I'm not much of a dancer." Other than alone in my bedroom, I add silently. But he doesn't need to know that.

He pulls me right back into his grip, holding me so close I can hear his heartbeat thundering in my ear. "Don't care. Dance with me." Then with one hand holding me close, and the other sliding down onto my ass, he leans into the crook of my neck and kisses it while we sway to the slow number the band is playing. For a second I tense, but something gives. Instead of pushing away, I press closer to him, even putting a soft kiss or two on his chest.

All the fight has gone out of me, and I can't seem to find it again. I've no idea how long we dance, but I'm snapped out of the moment when there's a bright explosion on night sky, illuminating us in reds and blues. My first thought is the Captain's tall pirate story, but it's only fireworks.

We look up, still standing close and swaying gently. Flash after flash lights up the deck, spraying every color imaginable into the air. The fireworks reflect in the crystal clear waters, making it seem like we're completely surrounded. It's magical. Something tells me that I need to remember this, because I can't imagine a more beautiful wedding, and no matter what happens afterwards, for right now, it's mine.

Captain Chuck comes by with fresh champagne flutes, giving us one each with a wink before returning to mingle with the other passengers. He's got the sense to leave us alone. Gavin downs his in one long gulp and then throws the glass overboard. "We're going upstairs."

I open my mouth to protest, but my body betrays me. I shiver in anticipation, and when I speak it's not the *oh my God, no* that I was thinking. Instead, I just say, "Okay." Grinning mischievously, I throw my glass like he did, watching it arc through the air until it disappears into the inky blackness surrounding the ship. I giggle like I've just done something ridiculously naughty.

Who are you and what have you done with Angie?

With a laugh, Gavin scoops me up in his powerful arms, carrying me easily. Instead of fighting him, I nuzzle my face against his broad chest and wrap my arms around his neck. My new husband might be an asshole, but there's still a stupid smile on my face.

The crowd cheers and claps as he carries me past them. I burst out laughing, and I can't stop it, burying my face in the crook of his neck in embarrassment. Everyone knows where we're heading, and why.

I've just gotten married to a guy who confuses, infuriates and tempts me like no other.

And it's time for the wedding night.

22 ANGIE

We burst in through the door to our suite, him carrying me over the doorstep, true to tradition. Sort of, anyway. I suppose most brides are carried over in more than a bikini, but at least it's white. I giggle, getting a look from Gavin. The champagne's still bubbling in my blood.

He kicks the door shut behind him, not bothering with the lights. Outside, the fireworks are still going off, throwing showers of colorful light spattering across our bedroom. I hardly notice. His eyes are locked to mine, gazing at me so intensely. My world narrows until it's just the two of us while he carries me to the bed.

It's going to happen. I should be scared, or

angry, or at least push him away, but I don't want to. What I want is *him*, at least for tonight.

He lowers me gently onto the white satin sheets, then follows until he covers me. His lips trail kisses along my shoulder and collarbone, as he pulls the flimsy wrap aside. It's like I'm viewing myself from the outside in, watching as I give myself to him. I don't know if the haze is alcohol or lust, but I can't stop touching him. I explore him with my hands, running them all over his muscular back, tracing his shoulder blades with my fingertips.

I have to taste him. Running my fingers into his hair, I grip him tightly and pull him up to me until our lips touch. For the first time ever, I'm the one kissing him, savoring the flavors of champagne and dessert, and something that's uniquely his.

Pressing against me, he forces his hips in between my legs, and even though we're still wearing our bathing suits, I can feel his hardness against me. "You have no idea how much I've wanted to do this," he says huskily.

"Shut up and kiss me, before I change my mind." I squirm, eager to finally ease the emptiness inside me.

He chuckles softly before he leans in and kisses me roughly, claiming me with his mouth. Then he moves, leaving me gasping while he licks and nibbles his way along my jaw. I'm holding my breath, just feeling his skin against mine.

As he travels down the side of my neck toward my shoulder, he grabs my bikini top and pulls it up. My breasts pop free, and he palms one with his big hand, squeezing it and rolling my nipple between his rough fingers. I moan in response, arching against him.

His lips explore my collar bone, kissing their way onto my chest. Every touch sends a little spark arcing across my skin. Slowly, but surely he approaches the rise to my unhandled breast until he closes his mouth around the nipple.

My racing heart feels like it's about to beat its way out of my chest while adrenaline courses through me, making me shiver so hard it almost hurts. Burying my fingers deep in his hair, I try to keep him in place when he kisses down the bottom curve of my breast, but no matter how hard I tug, he ignores me.

It's only when he gets as far as my belly button, swirling his tongue around it teasingly, that I realize where he's heading. I look down at him past my breasts, watching closely as he nibbles closer to the top of my bottoms. When he's almost there, he looks up and grins. It's his usual cocky smirk, but for once it doesn't annoy me at all. I want the promise of what that smug little smile holds.

Hooking his fingers in my bikini bottoms, he raises his eyebrows at me. A final, silent question. Swallowing deeply, my response is to raise my hips. He rips the bottoms off, leaving me naked except for the top hanging loosely around my neck. My breasts rise and fall in time with my rapid breathing as I wait to see what he's going to do.

Gavin puts his strong hands on the insides of my thighs and forces them wide. God, he can see all of me. *No one's* seen me open like this before. Not like this. Please, oh please, don't let him think I look weird down there or something.

He smiles. Not a grin or smirk, but a real smile. He's looking at me with a reverent expression on his face. "You're so fucking beautiful." He kisses me just above my mound, then down over my hip and onto the inside of my thigh, each touch building the anticipation just a little bit more. Closer and closer, until his lips are almost there, and then he switches to my other thigh and starts over. I fist the sheets in frustration while I watch him.

When I press my hips towards him, trying to get to the main event, he laughs softly. "You're so impatient, babe."

"I'm not your babe." I don't know why I bother to talk back. He has me right where he wants me, and I'm not going anywhere.

He kisses me right on the clit, and the only warning I get is his hot breath rushing over it a split second before. Oh my freaking God. A shock races through me, sending tingles all the way out to my fingertips. I can't believe how good this feels.

"Are you sure, *babe?*" Pulling back, he waits until I whimper and chase him with my hips. He laughs, then leans back in, swiping his tongue right up through my folds. Drawing a sharp breath through my teeth, I arch against his mouth. He's still a cocky jerk, but I'll tolerate him. For now.

He paints with broad strokes of his tongue, kissing and licking and driving me insane. Over the years I've gotten pretty good at getting myself off, but it doesn't even compare to the magic he's working between my legs. As molten heat roils around inside me, I realize how close I am.

My nerves kick into overdrive and my muscles lock up as I come hard on his tongue. He wraps his hands over my thighs, keeping me in place and driving my climax forward with his oh-so-talented mouth. I shake under him, and it feels like it's going to last forever. The fireworks have stopped outside, but now I'm seeing them on the backs of my eyelids.

When my body finally relaxes and eases back on the bed, I open my eyes to find him grinning at me, his eyes crinkled into crow's feet at the corners. He continues to place soft kisses on my folds, making me shiver deliciously with each one. Everything feels so freaking sensitive.

"How was that, *babe*?" he asks, obviously trying to get a rise out of me.

I close my eyes for a moment again, just concentrating on breathing. "I've decided, that if you keep doing that, you can call me babe all you want."

"Oh, I've barely started." He stands, and tugs down his swim trunks. For a moment they catch on the huge lump underneath, but he works them past, then stands before me in all his glory.

Wow.

His cock, and that's the only word I can think of that seems adequate, is huge. As he climbs back on the bed and in between my legs, it bounces softly in front of him. I lick my lips nervously, unable to take my eyes off it. Am I ready for this?

He hovers over me, resting his weight on his painted forearms at either side of my head, then looks down, watching my reaction. Bringing one arm back, he aims himself, sliding the broad head up and down between my folds. Each touch only adds to the boiling heat inside me.

I've never been more ready. I meet his gaze, locking my eyes to his. "Do it."

Nestling himself right at my entrance, he pushes slowly forward while he watches me intently. I draw a tight little breath when I feel him part me, pushing into me for the first time. He's so huge, or I'm so tight, that it aches, but God it feels good. As he opens me, I surrender to him, but I never look away from his intense, dark gaze.

His hips touch mine. He's all the way in. I've done it. No longer a virgin. My first time is on my wedding night, and my husband, who I spend half my time lusting after and half my time furious with, is going to be my stepbrother. I can't think about that, otherwise I'll freak out. I'm just going to live in the moment, and right at this moment, I'm filled by Gavin's long, thick cock.

"You alright?" His voice is soft, but with a hint of urgency to it.

I nod. "Yeah." I close my eyes and take a second to let the feel of him inside me drive away my concerns. "Yeah, more than alright."

"Good, 'cause I don't think I can hold still any longer."

He slides out almost as slowly as he went in, then returns a little faster. Again, a little faster. And again. I spread wider, inviting him. Soon he's thrusting in a regular rhythm, his tattoos dancing as he moves, while I writhe underneath him as his magnificent cock strokes me in all the right places.

We started out making love, but now he's fucking me, and I love it. I crave it. Our moans mingle as our sweaty bodies mash against each other. He takes me, and I meet him stroke for stroke, his tight abs flexing and his hard ass thrusting, fucking me like a piston.

Then he pulls out, leaving me whimpering, his cock slick and still hard as steel. "Turn around. Get on all fours."

In a daze, I obey, and as soon as I'm up, he grabs my thighs and pulls me to the edge of the bed so he can stand behind me. The height is perfect, and he slides smoothly back into me, making me groan deep in my throat.

I wasn't sure at first, but as soon as he reaches around and plays with my breast with one hand while he rubs my clit with the other I'm sold. He plays my body with the touch of a master, directing me exactly where he wants.

"Come for me, babe. Do it for me." His husky voice is tight with need. He pounds into me, the fronts of his thighs smacking into the backs of mine while his fingers work overtime. I'm overwhelmed by sensations, floating like I'm in a barrel, the edge of the waterfall roaring in my ears. He claims me, and much as I try to hold off, I can't.

I go over the falls.

Every muscle in my body clenches. My toes curl painfully and my back arches tightly as I come. I think my eyes are still open, but all I see is white as I shake beneath him. Tingles rush from my core to everywhere else in my shivering body. I've never felt anything like it.

Through all the quaking and groaning and tightening, he thrusts, driving wave after wave of pleasure through me. He's going to kill me. I've never felt anything so powerful, so over the top crazy. I scream. I don't know if we have any next door neighbors, but if we do they definitely know about us now and I can't find it in me to care.

I'm only just coming down when his thrusts get even faster and his breath grows erratic. With a deep, throaty groan, he pushes himself deep and I feel him fill me with heat, pulsing inside me. A tiny voice in the back of my mind yells that I should be panicking right now, but I don't hear it. Or I don't understand it. I don't know. All I know is that this is the most amazing feeling I've ever felt and I'm not about to let anything ruin it for me.

He finishes, and after one last pulse, he stops moving completely. For a moment, time stands still, then he collapses to my side, pulling me with him so we land in a spooning position. He never even slips out, holding me close.

And that's how we fall asleep.

23 GAVIN

My brain feels like I woke up in a zombie marching band apocalypse. Head pounding, stomach churning, mouth like sandpaper, and I can't feel my fingers. I try to roll over, but my arm's trapped by a soft, sleeping body. Curled into me, Angie's still fast asleep, and when I move it's like she senses it even in her sleep and inches closer until her face nuzzles my chest.

Holy fucking shit.

Little Miss Principles. The girl who wouldn't give me the time of day. The girl who said right to my face that she wouldn't even if I was the last man on the Earth. Sleeping in my arms. Well, if that's not a victory, I don't know what is.

Not just once, either. Once more in the middle of the night, and then again only a couple of hours ago. I know it must have been her first time, but once she let herself give in, she turned into a fucking wild cat. She damn near wore me out, which I'm never going to tell her, because I wouldn't hear the end of it.

But right now, when she's not busting my balls, she's adorable. Who am I kidding? Even when she's chewing me out, she's cute as hell. I don't know what it is about her. At first it was my pride. Hunting down the one who ran away. But, fuck, I love the way she challenges me, and she might deny it, but she enjoys it too.

Now? I don't have a fucking clue, but my victory doesn't feel like one. I'm not ready for our game to be over. Letting out a soft breath, I brush a lock of silky hair out of her face. I'm not used to not wanting to let go. Fortunately, we have some honeymoon left to screw it out of our systems. That should be enough.

Our honeymoon. I laugh softly. What the fuck have we gotten ourselves into? I might've dropped out of school, but it doesn't take a degree to know there's no way it's legal. Maybe we just got our parents hitched without them even knowing it. That'd be fucking rich. "Hey Dad. Guess what? You're married now. Congrats! I brought you a t-shirt."

I stroke her hair softly, just watching her breathe. The covers slipped down while we slept, exposing those perfect tits and I watch them rise and fall. I want to touch, but I don't want to wake her yet.

What's up with that, Gavin? You falling in love or something?

Wouldn't that be a nightmare? Angie's growing on me, though. I could stay here all day watching her like this. Unfortunately, I still can't feel my arm and I've got morning wood hard enough to drive in a nail. I need to take a leak something fierce.

When I gently pull my arm free, she stirs but doesn't wake up. Pins and needles race up and down from my fingertips to my shoulder. I mutter curses under my breath and shake it out until it stops tingling. She grabs a pillow and cuddles into it in her sleep, now that I'm not next to her anymore. The motion rolls her even further out from under the covers, exposing a soft thigh. I'd love to run my hand up it, right into her juicy little pussy, but first, nature calls.

I shut the bathroom door quietly and look down to find the bane and joy of my existence staring right back up at me. Fuck that shit, I just need to piss. After a bit of awkward positioning, I get my business done, then head into the shower. The hot water rushes over me, clearing out the booze fog from last night.

I just stand there a while, slowly waking up, half hoping that Angie's going to come in, but she never does. Man, that girl can sleep. Or maybe she's just waiting for me to come back. The thought gets me shutting off the water and grabbing my towel, my cock already firming back up. I wrap the soft terry cloth around my waist and I'm just about to open the door when I hear her voice.

"It was crazy!" She's on the phone. "I know. I couldn't believe it either. Still can't."

Shit. I have a bad habit of eavesdropping on her phone calls, but come on, we're sharing a room and she's talking about me. I can't *not* listen.

"Yeah, you would suggest that, wouldn't you? I'm not going to be able to walk normally today as it is." She giggles and I can hear her moving around on the bed, probably still naked. "God, it was wonderful.

Every time."

The satisfied tone in her voice makes me grin. Fuck, I'm tempted to stride out there, rip my towel off and take Angie right on the bed while her friend's listening, so she can get the experience firsthand. If I wasn't hard before, I'm more than fucking ready now.

"But seriously, you know I'm not on the pill."

At her words, my skin prickles as if the temperature in the room dropped ten degrees. Yeah, she was a virgin, but with the way we met and her plans for Paul, I'd have figured she was on the pill or depo or something. Didn't I ask last night? Fuck. How drunk was I? I never forget, and why the fuck wouldn't she have said anything?

Angie laughs a little nervously. "Yeah, right. He already thinks we're a bunch of gold diggers. Can you imagine? Talk about a strange family tree." She laughs again, but I'm failing to see the humor in their fucked up conversation. "Sure, you could be the nanny. Get them to set us up in an awesome house or something, Auntie Cassie. Yeah, being stuck with him would kind of be the downside. Maybe if we just stick to having sex and he keeps his mouth—"

That's enough. If she has more to say she can

say it to my face. I slam open the door, cold fury swirling in my gut. "Hang up."

Angie's face is as white as the sheets. "Cassie? I've gotta go. Later, okay?" She puts the phone down and holds up her hands. "I don't know what you heard, but—"

"Shut up." I close my eyes a second. When I open them again, she's looking at me, all cautious and worried and shit. The rational part of my brain knows I fucked up by not keeping it wrapped, but when I look in her eyes, all I see is every gold digger who's ever come sniffing at our door. "Why didn't you tell me? Why the fuck didn't you say anything?" I hiss.

She recoils from me, putting her back against the headboard and clutching the sheet to her chest. "Gavin…"

"What? Cat got your tongue?" Goddamn it. That warm fuzzy feeling? It was nice while it lasted. "You really had me going with that sweet, innocent act of yours." Even when she cringes away, I can't stop myself. "Wanna know a little more about your *husband*? Twenty-five years ago, *I* was the little slip-up that got my mother's claws into Dad's bank account and bought her a nice little house in the city. Laugh it up with your friend. I'm out." I pull clothes out of my suitcase and get dressed. I need to get out before I do anything stupid. Stupider.

Angie sits there staring at me in horror. "Gavin, I know what it probably sounded like, but I was just kidding. What are you—"

"You were kidding about not being on the pill?"

"No, but—"

"Kidding about being *stuck* with me?"

She has the grace to look guilty about that at least, but I don't hear any denials. I know what girls think of me, money and sex. I'm not in love with Angie, so why does it hurt so much when I hear her admit to being just like all the others?

"You think you're the first one to try it? You know what? It's my own fucking fault. I didn't even ask. You screwed up though, talking where I could hear you. Would've been safer to wait a few days. Could've had that many more chances to hit the jackpot. Wouldn't that have been fun?" I need to get the fuck out of here. I feel like such an idiot.

"Gavin!" She's crawling over the bed, looking drop dead sexy. "You're acting crazy. It was a mistake! We were drunk. I didn't even think about it, which was dumb, yeah, but we were both stupid. I was just nervous and joking with Cassie."

It would be easy to believe her. I've gotta get out of here before I head back in and fuck her again. Tears run down her face, but I'm not fucking falling for it. Not again. Pulling on my pants, I ignore her. A shirt, a pair of shoes, and I'm gone. This is exactly the kind of shit I was afraid of, and I should've fucking known better. Nobody is too cute, or too innocent when money's involved.

"I need some space. Do me a favor and stay out of my way. I'll do the right thing if I have to, but enjoy this honeymoon, because we're not having another one." I'm fucking growling, I'm so pissed.

My hangover is back, a painful spike hammering through my skull. Even as I tear open the door to the hallway, leaving Angie behind naked on the bed, all that flashes in my brain are memories from last night. Of her under me. On top of me. Of me fucking her deep and making her mine.

Fuck. I need a drink.

24 ANGIE

The door slams behind him, and I sag back on the bed, stunned.

What just happened? Irritation, panic, a joke about knocking me up on my wedding night. All of those I could have understood, but not that. He exploded. There's no other word for it. Does he really think I could do something like that? I knew when he made the comment about my mother's motivation that it was something he worried about, but me?

That's tinfoil hat level paranoia.

I can't take back last night, even if I wanted to. Even now, I don't know that I do. Last night was incredible. I'd never thought anyone would be able to make me feel like that. I didn't know it was possible to feel like that, but he made my first time magical. There's no way he didn't feel it too.

Shit.

I need someone to talk to. Joyce? I guess, if I wanted to hear about how the same thing happened with her second husband who was amazing with his toes. Pass. I blow my hair out of my eyes in frustration. Yes, that'd be great. How would I even start? "Hi there, inappropriate old lady, let me tell you about how I fucked my stepbrother and how awesome it was until he flew off the hook." I'm sure she'd love it.

I guess Cassie would be the obvious choice. Picking up the phone from my nightstand, I scroll until I find her name and tap the call button. It rings a bunch of times and I almost give up, but then I hear her familiar voice. "Angie! Are you alright?" She's concerned. I cut her off pretty suddenly before the argument.

I sigh. "Yeah. Or at least I will be." I think.

"Whoa, what happened? I heard Gavin in the background before you hung up, and he sounded really pissed."

I want to cry again, and it pisses me off that he

can make me feel that way. "Yeah, you could say that. He overheard us talking, and now he's convinced that I tried to get him to knock me up. Like I'm some gold digging slut. What the hell is up with that?" For once, Cassie's quiet. Like dead quiet, so long that I think I've lost my connection, except that I can hear her breathe. "Cassie? Are you there?"

"Yeah. Just not sure what to say. What a prick."

"Well, I mean, I guess what we said sounded bad, but—"

"Seriously? Making excuses for him?"

"No, I'm not. It's just—"

"Angie. Listen to yourself. You don't actually want him, do you?"

"No!" I say it way too quickly, too defensively, and she hears it. "But I might be pregnant. With him."

"I know it's scary, trust me, but Angie? We had our periods together like last week."

"Yeah, but—"

"But nothing. Chances are super slim. You're going to be fine."

"I suppose, but—"

"Even with the worst timing, once isn't very

likely."

"Um…" I'm only on the phone. I shouldn't be this embarrassed.

"So, not just once then. I knew it! He was good, wasn't he? How many times?"

She giggles, which annoys me. I sigh. "Cassie, priorities!"

"I'm sorry." She laughs. "Excuse me for wanting to dish with my first married friend. He's really getting to you, isn't he?"

"I'm not really married." Probably. Just the thought scares me a little. "He's an asshole, it's just—"

"You like him." Her teasing tone gets on my nerves. Maybe I shouldn't have called her after all. "You're in love with your totally hot asshole stepbrother, and now that he's mad at you, you don't want to admit it."

"He's inappropriate, crude, bossy, vulgar and a big freaking bully. You heard what he did to Paul." Anger is good. Anger means I'm not scared or hurt.

"And still you want him back so bad it hurts."

"Yeah. Wait, no! Stop putting words in my mouth." I should've gone looking for Joyce.

All Cassie does is laugh. "Alright, so tell me this, then. Why are you so upset right now? You got your nasty stepbro sex, and now he's pissed and out of your hair. Isn't that like having your cake and eating it too? Or maybe he was *that* good at eating *your* cake—"

"Cassie!"

She's trying to stifle her laughter. I can hear it. "Seriously. Why do you care, Angie? If you can answer that, maybe you can figure out what you need to do."

"I—"

"Yeah, I thought so. Think about it. Oh, and speaking of thinking about it, I just remembered that I *may* have given away that you're not here to your mom." She sounds mildly apologetic at that at least. "Sorry, I just didn't think about it, and you never actually asked me to cover for you…"

"Yeah, yeah." I sigh. I seem to do that a lot lately. "She was bound to figure it out eventually anyway. I'll worry about that when I talk to her next time."

"So what are you going to do?"

"About Mom?"

"No, silly. About your sexy-ass stepbrother with the big chest, sexy tattoos and the tight ass. That guy you married." She's laughing again.

"What can I do? He made it pretty clear that he doesn't want to see me. Maybe I'll just spend the day catching rays while I pretend that he never existed." Chances of that happening are just slightly higher than pigs flying.

"If you were me I might almost believe that." For a moment she's actually serious. "I know you Angie. You're not going to be able to let this go. When you first sink your teeth into something, you're like a freaking bulldog."

"Are you calling me a bitch?" I snort. "He doesn't want to see me, fine. I'll avoid him for a couple of days. I can do that."

She makes a frustrated sound. "Listen to me. It's like college, right? Once you decided you wanted to go to med school, everyone told you how hard it was, how difficult it was to get in. About how you'd have to do all these internships that don't pay, that you wouldn't have a social life, and on and on and on. Do you remember how no one believed you could do it?"

I remember. Even Mom was skeptical, and she's

always been all about me finding my own way. "You believed I could."

"Yeah, because I know you." She sounds like she's explaining things to a small kid. "You weren't giving up. It was always on your mind, even when you pretended it wasn't, and now you've been admitted. You're going to do it."

"Okay, but I don't see what that has to do with my asshole stepbrother." As soon as I mention him, flashes of his naked body standing in the shower with the water running over his perfect chest rush through my mind. Why does the guy I hate most have to be the one that can make me weak with just a thought?

"You sound exactly the same when you talk about him as you did when you were talking about med school. You're stuck on him. I'm sure you'll try to waste the day working on your tan, but you'll be spending all that time figuring out how to get him back into bed."

"Cassie!" It's a fake outrage, because I know she's right.

"It's true."

"He hurt me, Cass…" That's it. That's the worst part. That I'd finally opened myself up to him, completely, and the first time something came up, he turned it around and stabbed me in the heart with it.

"I know, hun," she whispers softly. "And if you talk to him, and he's still an asshole, I'll be here to help turn his balls into jerky, promise. But go talk to him. You're never going to be able to let it go until you do."

"I wish you were here."

"Me too. My tan is complete crap!" Her voice is back to teasing. "Go find him. Talk. Be the bulldog, not the bitch."

"I don't even know how to take that."

"You're worth a hundred pretty rich boys, Angie. I have to go, but I want a full report, alright? And if you guys aren't fucking on the regular by the time you get home, I'll eat my hat."

"Do you even own a hat?"

"I'll buy one. Later, sweetie. You're going to be okay."

"Later, Cassie." The line goes dead. Throwing myself backwards, I sprawl on the bed, my arms stretched wide while I stare straight up. My eyes follow the blades of the ceiling fan as they spin just quickly enough that it's difficult to keep up. Just like this trip. It's like I'm only barely hanging on, and I don't know if I can keep it up or if I'm getting spun right off.

A gust of wind blows in through the open door to the balcony, making me shiver. There's a bank of clouds on the horizon moving quickly towards us and the breeze is noticeably cooler than it was even before the phone call. Soaking up sun isn't even going to be an option today, is it?

Great.

I guess I'll be looking for my husband, then.

25 GAVIN

"Another." I raise my finger to get the bartender's attention. He's tall and lanky, wearing a white button-down shirt with those straps around the upper arms like the card dealers wear at casinos. After the bomb Angie dropped on me this morning, the idea of gambling kinda pisses me off.

He gives me a disapproving look down his long nose. "Are you sure? It's not even one o'clock. A little early to get in a party mood, isn't it?" He tries to put a friendly spin on it, but he's judging me. I can hear it. "Newlywed life that bad?" The bar's pretty empty at this hour, but the few people around to hear him, chuckle.

"I asked for a drink, not your opinion. Another."

The look he gives me is a mix of curiosity and disgust, but I don't give a fuck, and when he slides the scotch my way I take it with a nod, then ignore him.

I feel like an asshole. The pleading look on Angie's face when I left her is burned into my brain. Fine, so I suck at anger management. What am I supposed to do now? Crawl back and beg forgiveness?

A man's got his pride. Not that I'm so damn proud of myself right now. The doubts creeping into the back of my mind don't help either. Maybe I went over the top? Projecting Dad's paranoia? Fuck if I know.

Sliding my fingers along the edge of the bar, I play with the texture, feeling the bumps and nicks in the stained wood. Just distracting my fingers while my mind tries to work. I'm rationalizing, just because I was too drunk and lovesick to remember to wrap my pecker. Fuck.

Angie's not the first girl I've fucked and dumped. She's not the first to try and trap me with pregnancy shit either. I didn't make it out of fucking high school before our lawyers had to handle my first paternity test. Negative. Which she already knew, but that didn't stop her from trying.

And then there're the creeps with investment opportunities too good to pass up, so long as I act now. Just a few million, and we'll never have to work another day in our lives, they say like that's not my life already.

So I say sit back and use the users. If they want to fuck me, I'll give 'em a ride. If they want to wine and dine me, I'll gladly oblige. Just don't expect me to call in the morning. Not once have I felt bad about it. Until today.

Waking up next to Angie was different. The sun played over her naked body, golden light warming the hints of skin peeking out of the sheets like a naughty promise. Different? Fuck, it was awesome. So why does she have to just be like all the others? *Is she?* asks a distant voice in the back of my head.

Tipping back my glass, I drain it. Hair of the dog. Just what I needed to burn off what was left of my hangover. It's exactly what I need, because while I'm trying to let go of her, something in the back of my head isn't letting me, and the scotch helps me pretend not to care.

I try to drain my glass again, but nothing's

coming out. Right. Already did that. "Another." The bartender shakes his head again and I get ready to bitch him out when the world rocks. For a second I don't get what happened. Buzzed? Abso-fucking-lutely. World rocking drunk? Not even close. It's not until I see the bartender securing the glass racks and putting bottles away that I realize it's the ship rocking and not me.

Through the window I see thick clouds rolling towards us, not quite obscuring the sun, but soon. Looks like crappy weather's coming our way. Awesome. Suits my mood better anyway. I was getting a bit sick of all the happy people hanging out in their designer swimwear, lounging around happily on the sundecks talking in happy voices about how awesome everything fucking is. Because it's not.

"Gavin."

I don't turn to face the voice. Of course I recognize it. She sounds angry, disappointed and sad, all at the same time. How the hell am I supposed to respond to that? I've got enough going on in my own head, thanks.

When I don't answer, Angie slides onto the stool next to me. Having her near me drives me crazy, muscle memory remembering last night and eager to go again. She's wearing a flowery sundress that's sheer enough that in the right light, I bet I could see everything.

I want to tear it off to see if she's wearing anything underneath. Common sense says she is, but my imagination is convinced she isn't, filling my mind with images of fucking her right on top of the bar, in front of everyone. Hell, why shouldn't I? The damage is already done.

The bartender gives us a curious look but keeps his distance until she speaks to him. "Could I have two glasses of water, please?" She sounds cool and collected. A far cry from how I left her. Gone from molten heat to frosty ice.

"Sure thing, Mrs. Caldwell." We watch in silence as he pulls down two tall beer glasses, fills them with ice out of a bucket under the bar, then pours them full of water. With a practiced motion, he slides them down the bar just like he did with my scotch. "I'd keep a hand on them, though. The seas are getting choppy out there." After seeing us catch, he moves to the other end of the bar, pretending not to watch us.

"Thank you." Taking one glass for herself, Angie

pushes the other towards me. "Unless you want to feel even more miserable after you're done feeling miserable, you should drink some water." I watch her sip hers but I don't touch mine. It's a stupid kind of spiteful pride.

Minutes drag by without either of us saying anything. What does she want? An apology? She's not getting it. Not unless I'm sure, and I'm not good at that apologizing shit anyway. I can't blame the cruise on her, or our crazy fucking wedding, but for all I know she just grabbed the perfect opportunity.

Fuck, that sounds lame even to me.

"So tell me. What do you want?" I lash out at her like a wounded animal. "Money for college? A house in France? A diamond-studded hobby horse? Can't put a price on love, can you? But a baby on the other hand... gold mine."

She stiffens, but doesn't answer. Just nurses her water, ignoring me in a way that I can't ignore. Every minute she spends *not* looking at me is a minute I want to grab her chin and force her to look in my eyes. Quiet Angie is new. I don't know her, and I don't like her. Give me ball-busting Angie any day.

Finally, after what feels like an eternity, she opens

her mouth. "I want…" Dragging it out. No idea if she's still thinking or just baiting me. "I want you to get the fuck over yourself." There she is. The bitch is back. Good.

"Me? That's fucking rich. You can drop the act now, babe. You won." I reach for the water then change my mind, refusing to take anything from her. Instead, I do what I do best. Lash out again. "Will you name him after me, at least?"

She keeps her voice even, but her fists tighten until her knuckles turn white. When she looks at me, cold fury stabs at me from her narrowed eyes. "I don't know what people have done to you. Maybe they've been horrible. Maybe you have every right to be suspicious, but maybe you're just so freaking full of yourself that you can't see past your own damn nose."

"Angie—"

She cuts me off. "Shut up. I'm not done." It's not just fury. There's a sadness in her eyes as well. "But when you blow up and blame me for a stupid mistake—which for the record is as much yours as it is mine—like I'm out to get you, that doesn't make you a freaking victim. It just makes you petty and small."

"You don't fucking know me." I hiss it out through clenched teeth, hating how I sound like a whiny kid. The pain inside still wants to get out, and impulse control's never been my strong suit. "You have no idea what my life's been like. Don't fucking judge me."

Sipping her water, she takes her sweet time. Is she doing it on purpose to aggravate me? She doesn't even look at me when she speaks. "I feel sorry for you."

"Me? Well, don't. I don't need your fucking pity."

"You spend so much time hiding from attachment that you don't recognize it when it slaps you in the face. No wonder you only do one-night-stands. You're too much of a fucking chicken." She slams her empty glass on the counter and stands. Turning towards the door, she doesn't look at me when she speaks with a tight voice. "You know, for one night I thought I'd found the real you. The little part inside that's not an asshole. Guess the joke's on me. Turns out that little part's an asshole too."

And with that, she strides right out, leaving me

with my empty glass of scotch and an untouched glass of water. She's almost outside when I go after her, except the ship picks that moment to roll again, and I'm too stiff and tipsy to compensate. I stumble against the counter and grab on to stay upright.

Fuck.

By the time I'm moving, she's gone and the other patrons are pointedly looking away.

Fuck.

I slam my fist in the counter, getting a small amount of pleasure out of watching the others jump. Then I grab the glass of water she gave me and chug it all down, to the last drop. Even that gets me thinking of last night. Of sweat and sweet promises, all in the heat of the moment. Why can't I hate her? I don't want this heavy feeling in my chest. Maybe she doesn't want to be stuck with me, but I sure as hell seem to be stuck with her.

Fuck.

Throwing the glass on the floor, I smile thinly at the loud crash as it shatters into a starburst of tiny shards. I get up again, my shoes crunching as I walk over the floor, my gaze straight forward, and this time I don't stumble. But I don't meet anyone's gaze on the way out either.

26 ANGIE

When I get back to the room, the skies are dark and there's a slight patter of rain on the windows. Nothing big, but enough that I won't be doing my moping out on the balcony. The fan's blowing too much cool air now that the sun isn't baking our room through the windows, so I shut it off. The only noise left is the dull hum of the engines.

The whole room reminds me of Gavin, but where else would I go? I can't even take a nap without thinking about what happened in the bed. What a cruel twist of fate that the person who knows my body so well, doesn't seem to know me at all. We fit so perfectly together, and now everything's a mess.

I hate that he's an asshole, and I hate how even

now I'd forgive him if it meant feeling like we did last night again. Briefly, I consider taking one of the chairs and jamming it up against the door knob. If he can't get in, I can't be tempted to forgive him, but I don't. It's his room too, and even if he's an asshole, I don't have to be. I just want to.

We're supposed to eat at the captain's table again tonight, but I can't. No way. I barely held it together at the bar, and I'm sure everyone on board who might care knows about our fight by now. If I have to play the happy wife, I'll probably drive a fork through his leg before the main course shows up. The mental image of smiling at Captain Chuck while Gavin clutches his bleeding leg makes me snort humorlessly. *No, Angie! Bad idea.*

I'll just get room service or something. Or sleep. Lie here and cry while I plan more ways to hurt Gavin. I don't even know. For now I just stare at the ceiling, thinking about last night. There's a fleck of paint missing. Ugh, noticing that feels like a pathetic new low.

LL Cool J shouts out from my purse, startling me out of my daydreaming. I almost don't get it. I'm busy being miserable here in bed, and the phone is all the way over there. It doesn't stop though, so with a sigh, I get up on my elbows. I blow my bangs out of my face. Time for a trim. Just one more thing not going my way. Rolling to the edge of the bed and reaching over, I barely reach the fancy purse, grimacing when I remember who bought it for me.

Might as well get it over with. The suck is strong with me today. I tap the button and put the phone to my ear. "Hi, Mom."

"Angela! Where are you? And don't give me that Cassie crap. She let the cat out of the bag."

I get that she's annoyed, but I'm an adult. She's probably mostly hurt I lied. I suppose I'd be too. "Sorry, Mom. I'm…" I draw a deep breath. "I'm on a cruise."

There's silence for a long moment. "A cruise? How did you… Wait, did you take Herb's tickets?"

"Yeah. I know I shouldn't have, but it seemed such a shame to just throw them out."

She tsks. "I thought so too, but you didn't have to be sneaky about it. Why didn't you just tell me?" Yup, she's hurt. She's using that disappointed Mom voice. Everyone's mom has one, the one that makes you feel guilty no matter what you did. It's actually been a while since I've heard it.

"Honestly? I thought you'd be mad. I mean, they weren't ours to use."

"*Ours*? Honey, who're you there with?" There's an edge in her voice, though I don't know why. "I know it's not Cassie, so don't even try to lie."

"I'm here with Gavin. He found out I was going and came along. His name is almost the same as Herb's so they just figured we were you guys." That's the short version anyway.

Mom is quiet, but I can practically hear her thinking over the phone. "This is going to sound strange, honey, but did anything... odd happen? On the cruise I mean?"

Oh, no way. She knows?

I throw myself back on the bed, finding the missing paint spot on the ceiling while I decide how to answer. "You mean like, accidentally marrying my new stepbrother?"

She squeaks out a choking laugh. "Did—Did you guys go along with it?"

Oh God. My voice is tiny. "Yes."

There's a long silence, and I'm starting to panic. Then she sobs and my chin starts to quiver. Except it's not a sob, it's laughter. Like, can't catch your breath, stomach aching laughter. It's so loud it's hurting my ears, and I hold the phone away, staring at it like it's going to bite me. Now I know how Gavin felt the other day.

"Seriously, Mom?"

Then suddenly she stops, and I risk putting the phone close again. "I'm sorry!" She gasps for breath. "I know I should be mad, but I just wish I could've seen your faces when they… wait a minute. How far along with it did you go?"

My face gets so hot I can feel my phone stick against my cheek. "Well, here comes the bride, do you take this man, eating cake… dancing… You know, the works." I can't believe I told my mother I accidentally got married and she *laughed at me!*

"Mmhmm." She hears the words I'm not saying too. The consummation. "Does this have anything to do with our other conversation? I can't say I'm sorry to see Paul go, but rebounding with Gavin? Honey, I know he isn't actually your brother, but that's bound to get awkward."

"Awkward?" Understatement of the year. "You could say that. Aren't you more worried about the married part?"

"Did you sign anything?"

"No, at least I don't think so. Unless Gavin did." I try to remember, but I'm pretty sure we were whisked straight to the reception.

"If you didn't, then there is no marriage. Even if you did, the license was in our names. You might give a lawyer somewhere a headache, but I think you're in the clear," she says gently. Just listening to her voice and getting it off my chest makes me feel so much better. Adult or not, sometimes I need my mom. "But back to you and Gavin. Is this serious?"

"Of course not!" But I wish it was, something I won't admit even to her.

"I'm not surprised. He doesn't worry me like that Paul character, but he looks like he'd charm the booties off the Thanksgiving turkey if you left them alone together. Handsome too." She sighs. "Like father, like son. They apparently like us Wilson girls. Or did."

"How do you know we argued?" Is it that obvious?

"Oh Honey, I didn't. I was talking about Herb and me." Suddenly all the humor is gone from her voice.

"Wait, what? What happened?" I can't believe the same couple I saw the other night is already in trouble. No matter how I feel about how fast they've moved, I want it to work for Mom's sake.

She sighs again, sounding exactly like I've been feeling the last couple hours. "Remember when I told you about the secret investor? Turns out it wasn't Herb. I don't know who it was, or why they did it, but now Herb thinks I used our relationship to talk someone in his company into giving me the money. But I have no idea who did it if it wasn't him."

"And now he thinks you're just another gold digger." They really are like father, like son. "Well, that's about what Gavin thinks of me too, if it makes you feel any better."

"The Caldwells are a pair of grade A bastards."

My eyes go wide. She *never* swears. "Well, it's their loss. Screw him. Screw them. Screw the whole Caldwell Enterprises and its paranoid owners." Misery loves company, but company makes me feel better, too. We'll get through this.

"Language, Angie." Mom's voice is stern.

"Seriously, Mom?"

She breaks into laughter. "Oh, God no. Fuck'em."

"Mom!" Now I can count on two fingers the number of times I've heard her swear. I can't believe she just said that.

"Angie? They're breaking our hearts. It's worth a little swearing. Love sucks, but we have each other and we've made it through far worse." She sounds sad and resigned. I hate that someone has done that to her and I can't even hug her. We're both silent. I have no idea what to say, but then Mom speaks. "Hey, do you have TV? Wi-Fi?"

What? "Yeah, of course. This is a luxury liner, after all. All the comforts of home sweet mansion." I put all the snootiness into my voice that I can while I put my nose in the air. I'm pretty sure that's required, even when pretending. "Only the best champagne, the best caviar and every television channel on the planet."

"Alright, then we're doing girls' night over the phone. Order up some popcorn from room service and I'll find a movie to stream. Something good to moon and cry over. I'm just going to run and get mine popping." There's a thunk as she puts her phone on the table.

I plug my phone in so it won't run out of juice, and call room service. They seem a bit confused by my order for root beer and popcorn, but they do their job. Fifteen minutes later, Mom and I are watching Love Story, which is like, so ancient Leo wasn't even born, but I decide a young Ryan O'Neil more than makes up for it.

Girls' night over the phone is completely ridiculous, but it does the trick. It's not quite like being huddled up on the couch at home, but with our phones on speaker mode, it sort of works. The sound's a little funny when it's coming from two places at once, but it's really about us hanging out the best we can. Reminding each other that there is life outside of the male ego. Who knew I needed to take a cruise for some mother-daughter time?

When the movie's over, we call it a night. Next month's phone bill is going to hurt, but she totally made me feel better. At least for a while. Hopefully I did the same for her.

Crawling into bed, I wonder what Gavin's up to. Did he eat dinner with the Captain? It's almost eleven, so they should be done by now. Is he coming back at all? The thought of him flirting with someone else, maybe even going back to her room, brings tears to my eyes but I refuse to cry. I throw a pillow and a blanket on the couch just in case. More to make it obvious I'm not sharing the bed than to be nice.

My eyelids droop as soon as my head hits the pillow. I didn't do much today, but emotionally, it's been exhausting. Our birth control mistake, the fight, the *other* fight, finding out the Caldwells just have an asshole gene in the family tree somewhere. There's been a lot to take in.

If I think too hard my chest still aches, and the bed feels cold and empty, but the sound of rain pounding against the windows lulls me to sleep.

27 GAVIN

I cling to the rail of the front deck while the Golden Emperor of the Seas climbs one wave, then plunges over it, diving into the trough between swells, salty spray washing over me and threatening to knock me off my feet. Man versus nature. It's raw and wild, and simpler than dealing with whatever the fuck is going on with me and Angie.

Rolling my head, I try to work the massive kink out of my neck. I should've ignored the bed stuff on the couch and climbed right in with her. Slid close behind her and made her mine again.

Except fuck me if I could do it when I saw her lying there. Sleeping, her face was relaxed and peaceful so I let her be. Look at me, actually containing my fucking urges, instead of fucking up. Again.

While we're climbing the next wave, I risk letting go with one hand to brush hair out of my eyes. It's plastered to my skin, soaked and sticking. We crest again, rushing down into the next valley. I scream into the storm, letting the wind and salty spray rip away my frustration.

Last night I almost didn't go back. It would've been so easy to let some other gold-digger take me back to their room to fuck away my sorrows. Except I can't stop thinking about her, and it drives me crazy. Her face when I accused her, her eyes when she walked away from me in the bar, her mouth stretched wide in ecstasy as my cock slid into her the first time.

She's got a fucking free ride to Stanford, for Christ's sake. And she actually wants to go. With that kind of drive, why the hell would she want a baby? And what does she need me for? It doesn't fit, but it's a lot easier to be suspicious than it is to open myself up to a lifetime of the shit my dad's ex-wives throw at him.

But what if I fucked up? It's not like I didn't pack enough condoms to keep her happy until long after the cruise is over. I didn't ask, and it pisses me off that this mess is as much my fault as hers. I hate fucking up.

What if Angie's exactly what she looks like? A girl book-smart enough to get into med school, but naive enough to date a drugged up loser and only see the best in him. And maybe even worse, trust an asshole like me. What is it my anger management counsellor used to say? *Gavin, you're projecting. You need to let it go.* Dr. Meriam's voice sounds in my head like she's standing right next to me. If she is, I hope she's as fucking soaked as I am.

Everything brings me back to Angie.

Except my feet. It's not like she'll give me the fucking time of day now, even if I tried. But I want to see her. Touch her. Forget the last day and get back to what we had the other night. After we got married. I laugh, and spit out the mouthful of rain that comes with it. I've done some crazy shit, but nothing that compares to this trip.

Fuck, we had so much fun before this mess. I did at least. The teasing, the war of the words. All that delicious tension. Angie loved it too. She can't tell me she didn't. I carried her to bed that night, and when we finally came together it was fucking explosive. She rode my cock like it was made for her, and just thinking about it makes me hard.

A wave catches me full in the face, taking my breath away. It's getting rougher out here. I love the storm, but I'm not fucking stupid. It's time to get back inside before I get washed overboard. That'd be a shitty end to this trip. I wait for the next dip, then as soon as the spray passes me, I move, holding on to anything I can find as I go.

Which is a pain in the ass with a hardon. Shit. Even out in the storm, I can't clear my head of Angie. I hear her voice so clearly over the thrum of the waves that it's almost like she's really out here.

"Help!"

Wait a fucking minute.

28 ANGIE

I wake up just like I went to bed. Alone.

In the front room, the blankets are half on the couch and half on the floor. I try to pretend it doesn't matter, but knowing he was here last night makes me feel a little better. Only a little though, because he's gone again, and he never said a word. Did he check on me? Did he even care?

The floor heaves beneath my feet and I grab the wall for support. My stomach lurches right along with it, cutting off my train of thought. I remember that yesterday the lower levels felt more stable, so I head down to get something to eat and hopefully settle my stomach. I really hope I'm just seasick.

Something about riding the elevator in this

weather terrifies me, so I take the stairs, clinging to the handrails all the way down. I'm starting to get why Mom hates boats. I thought ships this big were supposed to be pretty stable, but I guess when the weather gets bad enough, all bets are off. Still, just being out of the room and having a focus is helping. I'm already less likely to empty my stomach in the stairwell.

I reach the mid-decks, and the rocking's a lot less pronounced. I'm just passing a porthole when movement draws my attention out in the rain. A flash of color moving down the deck towards the bow. Someone's out there in this weather? I squint, trying to make out the shape. There *is* someone out there, a faint shadow weaving unsteadily away, but it looks like a dress fluttering in the wind, and... a walker? Mabel? Where's Joyce?

Panic crushes what's left of my seasickness. I need to help her, or whoever that is. There's no way she's getting back on her own, and I couldn't live with myself if something happened to her because I didn't act fast enough. Well, it's not going to happen. I'm going out there.

I brace against the heavy door, pushing it open

with effort. I can barely do it when the weather's good. With the wind against me, I almost don't manage. How did Mabel get out there? It doesn't make sense, but that doesn't matter right now. Stepping out into the driving rain, I pull up the hood on my sweatshirt, only to have it ripped right back off by the wind. After a couple tries, I give up. Everything's soaked already, anyway.

Holding on to anything I can find, I make my way towards the staggering figure, but it's moving too fast. It's the wind, blowing her away. Her wheels must be sliding on the wet deck. Jesus. I try to move faster without losing control myself. Bending low, I half run along the rail.

She seems impossibly far away.

Shit, shit, shit.

I'll have to risk it. For a moment, I squeeze my eyes shut and draw a deep breath, then I let go, charging after her while the deck tips scarily beneath me. Whenever I can, I grab onto something to steady myself, but even then I almost go down a couple of times.

I'm getting closer, but as if in slow motion, I watch her finally lose control and fall. The metallic crash of her walker is barely audible through the storm. Steeling myself, I rush forward as quickly as I can, adrenaline giving me strength.

I pray I'll be able to get her back on her feet.

It's only when I'm almost there that I realize what an idiot I am. Collapsed on the deck is a serving cart with a ripped parasol, knocked over by the wind, its wheels still spinning. I grab the slippery railing, half laughing, half sobbing. I just put my life in danger for a rogue piece of deck equipment. My only consolation is that nobody saw me, because now that I'm closer, it doesn't look anything like a person.

The ship crests a wave and crashes down towards the next one, and only my death grip on the railing keeps me from going on my face. Shit, I might be in trouble. Now *I'm* the crazy person out in the storm, and the door isn't even visible from this far forwards. I need to get inside before I'm launched overboard.

I give the cart a frustrated glare before I start the long journey back. God, I feel stupid. I think the storm agrees with me. With the wind in my face, it seems even angrier than it was on the way out, and my knuckles whiten on the rail while I try to keep my footing.

Hand over hand, I pull myself along, keeping my eyes firmly on the shadowy outline of the center of the ship. I got out here. I can get back. Doing my best to convince myself while the wind and rain tear at my face and the crashing of the sea roars in my ears, I drag myself closer, step by step.

Either the storm is getting worse, or my arms are getting tired. Every wave that spills over the railings puts me that much closer to losing my footing and going down. I'm so wet and cold that it hurts, and my grip is getting weaker. I grit my teeth in determination, but part of me just wants to sit down and give up.

I can do this.

Someone once told me that every seventh wave is bigger when it washes up on shore. As a kid, I used to count them on the beach, running up the sand every time I got to seven, expecting it to come rushing further than the ones before. Sometimes it did, and sometimes it didn't, but maybe I was counting them wrong. It must be a seventh wave that suddenly washes over the ship, tearing my feet out from under me and ripping my grip loose from the railing.

I scream and my mouth fills with water. Scrambling for anything to hold on to, I get my fingers around the legs of one of the deck-mounted tables, but not without banging my forearm against one of the others. That's going to bruise in the morning, but bruises heal. Getting washed off the side of the ship? Much worse. Crawling under the table, I wrap both of my arms around the leg and cling to it for dear life. I'd hoped I'd get a little cover, but the rain's going straight sideways. Doesn't matter. There's no part of me left that isn't completely drenched.

Now what? I'm close enough that I can almost see the door, but new waves rush by, and I don't think I can manage to actually walk the rest of the way. So near, and yet too far. I don't know what to do, so I cry for help. No one's going to hear me, but I have to try.

"Help!" The first time, all I get is a mouthful of brine that cuts the sound right off. Sputtering and coughing, I spit, trying to get the raw taste of it out of my mouth. I try again, this time waiting for a wave to pass by before I yell. "Help!"

I don't know who I expect to answer. A guardian

angel? A crew member taking a walk in the stormy weather? Captain Chuck? I guess I expect nothing, which is exactly what I get. My voice is lost in the rumble of the storm, carried away by the wind. If someone was standing right in front of me, I'm not sure they'd hear me. It's only the refusal to give up that millions of years of evolution have instilled in me that keeps me yelling until my throat hurts.

No one is coming. I need to save my strength and try it on my own, before I give up and let go. I'm soaked clean through and my teeth are chattering. My eyes sting, and I can't tell if it's the rain or my frustrated tears. The door seems impossibly far away, but I need to make it.

It's now or nothing. Drawing a deep breath, I let go of the table and shimmy out into the open. Getting to my feet, I cling to the wall next to me, trying to keep my legs from giving out.

I'm never going to make it. Yes, you will. I refuse to end up a tragic footnote in the next issue of 'Cruising Life'.

Right. I swallow the huge lump in my throat and square my shoulders. Just one last burst of energy, then I'll be safe. All I need to do is get inside, then I can go back upstairs, take a nice warm shower and pretend this whole thing never happened. Everything's going to be perfect, or at least no more messed up than it was.

You can do this, Angie.

I go. Running into the wind, it feels like Poseidon's cold, wet hands are trying to pull me back. I get at least two, maybe three steps, before a wall of water crashes over me and knocks me off my feet. I should've counted to seven.

The hard deck knocks the air out of my lungs as I go right on my back. Streaks of pain ratchet through me, making me cry out.

More bruises. Not like it'll matter if I don't get back inside. I'm not sure how, when I can't even get back on my feet. My fingers look for handholds, but there's nothing, and for several long moments I lie there, buffeted by the water rushing along the deck and trying not to cry. I'm not doing a very good job of it. My eyes close.

Something clutches at my upper arm, and I panic. Images of giant octopi and sharks flash against the insides of my eyelids. I scream, but the grip doesn't let go, instead pulling me closer. Instinctively,

I struggle, until I hear the voice. *His* voice.

29 ANGIE

"Jesus, Angie. Calm the fuck down. I'm just trying to help. Unless you hate me so much you'd rather drown." Not waiting for me to answer, Gavin gets an arm under my armpit and pulls me up close.

I cry and cling to him, too exhausted and relieved to even think about being mad at him. "What are you doing here?" My throat is raw, and even this close I'm not sure he can hear my raspy voice.

"How about we talk about that later, when we're not being washed around and your lips aren't quite so blue, alright?" Wrapping one arm tightly around me, he grabs the wall next to us for support and pulls both of us up like my extra weight is nothing. Icy water rushes past us across the deck. "Can you stand?"

I don't answer right away, because I have no idea. I grab his arm, clinging to it for support while I test my legs. When they don't immediately give out, I swallow and nod.

"Good. We're going to walk slowly together, alright? I'll hold along here, and you hold on to me. I've got you." His voice is calm, and I use it to center myself. If he can keep his cool, then I will too. He leans in and speaks in a lower voice. "Are you ready?"

I draw a deep breath, then nod. Surprisingly enough, I trust him.

Without a word, he starts to move, nearly carrying me with him. Water spray and strong winds tear at me as we move slowly forwards. I support myself with my legs and balance as well as I can, but I'm pretty sure that even if I were unconscious he'd still carry me in. Even through our clothes, I feel the strength of him as he brings me to safety.

Several long, wet moments later, he pulls open the door. Its hinges squeak in protest and the wind does its best to slam it shut again, but he grunts and holds it in place, ushering me in ahead of him. As soon as I'm inside, I collapse against the wall, sliding down to the floor, my forehead resting on my shaking knees. My heart's jackhammering in my chest and my whole face tingles. I can't help it. I start to sob.

The door shuts with a slam, and I look up through saltwater and tears to see Gavin engaging the lock. His clothes cling to him like a second skin, and especially his t-shirt looks painted on. Even more than usual, I mean.

He turns, his face hard and his hair plastered to his skin. "What the fuck were you doing out there? You could've gotten hurt." The calm is over, and now the storm has moved inside.

"I—I thought I saw Mabel out there. I was just trying to..." I sob. "I was just trying to help her, but it was a stupid serving rack, and then the waves got stronger and I didn't count to seven and I slipped and—" A hiccup shakes my chest and I draw in a ragged breath.

"Never mind. Save your strength." The anger has left his voice. When I open my eyes again to look at him, all I see is concern and relief. "You can tell me later."

And with that, he scoops me up like a little kid and carries me. At first I want to tell him to let go of me, and that I'm still mad at him, but the words die unspoken. Instead, I wrap my arms around his neck and rest my face against the warmth of his chest. His shirt's still wet and sticky, but I can hear his heartbeat through it and that feels too good to ruin by arguing.

He heads straight for the elevator, keeping his feet even with the rocking of the ship. The idea of being trapped in an elevator during the storm still scares me, but I trust his judgement and he doesn't hesitate, hitting the call button. The doors open immediately. Most people are keeping in their staterooms today.

We ride up in silence, and he never lets me go. I'm pretty sure I can stand just fine on my own now, but I don't say anything. I remember the last time he carried me. It was over the threshold on our wedding night. With all my heart I wish I could relive that night instead of the bickering and accusations that will probably begin as soon as he puts me down.

Our suite's a mess. The room service cart from last night has fallen over, scattering popcorn, napkins and what was left of the melted ice. The rocking's worse up here, but not as bad as I remember from this morning. Maybe the storm is settling.

I push at his chest, and squirm a bit expecting him to put me down, but instead he brings me right into the bathroom, sets me on the floor and starts the shower. "We need to get you warmed up. Don't take this the wrong way, babe, but you look like hell."

A glance in the mirror leaves me speechless. I don't know if I'd say hell, but it's not my finest moment. "Yeah well," My teeth clack together as a shiver runs through me. "You aren't exactly a catch either. Unless it's the catch of the day."

He laughs and bends down, unzipping my hoodie. "I can't gawk at you in the shower if you're wearing all these things."

And here I thought I'd be glad if I never saw that smirk again. It actually makes me smile.

"Hey." I protest, but weakly, my teeth still chattering. I'm pretty sure I can undress myself just fine, but it feels nice when he does it. We aren't arguing yet, and I want to enjoy the feeling for as long as I can.

He drops my hoodie on the floor with a wet plop, then pulls me gently to my feet. I shiver in front of him, only my bra covering my top half. His gaze darkens as he takes in my breasts, but he's all business as he hooks his fingers into my sweatpants and yanks them off along with my panties. Blood rushes to my face and my flush battles the residual cold from the wind and rain.

"Turn around," he orders.

I clutch my arms in front of me and obey mechanically, until he stops me with his hands on my upper arms. He unlatches my bra and slips it off. I half expect him to grope me as he does, but he's a perfect gentleman. "Alright, in you go." The gentleman act goes right out the window when he lands a sharp smack on my ass to get me moving.

I forget to be annoyed when the hot water streams over me. God, that's good. Two days ago I'd have said better than sex, but now I'm not so sure. I tilt my face up at the showerhead, the warm water streaming over my skin a welcome change from the stinging rain outside. For several long moments, I forget about anything else.

30 ANGIE

I snap out of it when I hear the shower door open and close behind me. I sense him just before I catch him out of the corner of my eye.

He's naked, and I'm not sure how to feel about that. Nothing has changed, including the way I react to him. Except now that I know how he can make me feel, the heat of the shower is nothing compared to the heat that's pooling between my legs. Even so, the last time we were in the room together he pretty much called me a gold digging slut. My whole body tenses at the memory.

"My clothes were soaked too," is all I get in explanation. He's got a washcloth, which he reaches past me to get wet before he douses it in shower soap.

"Stand still." So close behind me that we're almost touching, he begins to scrub my back and shoulders.

I feel weak for letting him do this before we've resolved anything, but my muscles slowly relax and I don't say a word. Is it his way of apologizing? It's not nearly enough, but damn if it isn't half convincing me. I've had far, far worse apologies.

The cloth slips lower, until he's running it over my hips and my ass. Down the outsides of my thighs and over my calves. He even gets my feet, making me giggle when it tickles, before he slides back up along the insides of my legs. Definitely weak, but I can't find it in me to care.

When he starts to wash the insides of my thighs, I spread my legs a little without thinking about it. He soaps almost all the way up, but not quite, then stands. "Turn around, babe."

I swallow. Am I ready for this? We have so much we need to talk about, but would it hurt to just let this happen? One more perfect moment to remember from a trip of confusion and heartache. I should say no, but I turn to face him.

As soon as Gavin comes into view, my eyes eat him up. He's standing straight, his muscular, decorated body wet and flushed from the steam in the shower. I can't hide my desire quickly enough, and the corner of his mouth turns up. It's not the only thing that's up. His cock is pointing at the ceiling, swaying slightly with his movements. A shiver runs through me when I remember the magic of feeling it inside me. It had to be magic for something that big to fit, right?

"I'm sure you're still pissed as all hell at me," he says quietly.

I shake my head. Not in denial, but I don't want to think about that. Not right now.

He begins to scrub, first my left arm. "I can't help myself. You drive me crazy, babe." The rough cloth leaves a soft tingle in its wake as he moves from one arm to the next.

"I'm not your babe," I whisper.

"You're naked in my shower with my hands all over your body. I'm just calling it like I see it… babe."

His hands move to my shoulder blades, rubbing slow, soapy circles along my chest just above my breasts. My nipples respond, hardening into shameless little points. Traitors. When he slides the cloth down between them, he leans in and whispers hotly in my ear. "You make me so fucking hard." This close, I can smell his musk even over the flowery scent of the soap. It's heady, making me just a little woozy. He steadies me with his hands. "Do you need to sit down?" At first he sounds concerned, but then he adds while soaping my breasts, almost as an afterthought, "And while you're down there…"

Good to know some things don't change. "Are you sure? I have pretty sharp teeth, *babe*." I emphasize the last word sarcastically.

He only laughs, crouching to wash my thighs and hips. I'm very conscious of him being face to face with my pussy, but he doesn't seem to notice, concentrating on my legs. His touch is so soft, sliding smoothly through the sudsy soap that covers me.

Suddenly he leans forward and puts a kiss right on my mound, just above my clit. I squeak and jump, but his hands grip my hips to hold me in place. "Easy, tiger. I think it's time to rinse." He grins mischievously when he stands.

Grabbing the showerhead, he detaches it so he can spray me clean. Starting at my shoulders, he works his way down my body, passing the head close to my skin. The temperature is just on the edge of comfort, tingling without burning. He runs it right over my spine, making me gasp as the stream pounds against my lower back. Up and down my legs and over my ass, and then the insides of my thighs, letting it jet over my pussy for just a moment. I draw a sharp breath, but I stand still, waiting.

He moves the head to my front, but stays behind me, reaching around. Starting at my throat, he rinses my chest down towards my breasts, tickling my nipples rock hard with the pressure. I can't help myself and push back against his naked body.

Gavin's broad chest is like a wall, and his hardness slides against the small of my back. I wiggle against him, loving the feel of his skin against mine. His free arm goes all the way around below my breasts, clutching me to him while he moves the showerhead lower.

"That's right," his gruff voice rumbles next to me. "Rub yourself against me. So soft and sexy."

Ashamed at being caught out, I try to think of some glib remark, but his hand cups my breast, catching the nipple between his thumb and index finger. When he rolls it, I moan, reply forgotten.

He puts the showerhead right between my legs. The powerful stream rushes against my clit, burning with heat, thrumming against the sensitive nub. I writhe in his grasp, but he holds me tight. So good, but so much at the same time.

Sparks of pleasure arc out from my center, making my skin tingly and hot. Between his solid grip on my breast and the showerhead, he's got me right where he wants me and he's merciless. Usually I need to ease into it, but maybe I was just so worked up already, because the steady rush of water sets off a chain reaction.

"Come for me. Show me how fucking beautiful you are when you come." His voice is husky with need, sounding so damn sexy. The constant spray, the sound of his voice, his touch on me—they all combine to push me over the edge, and I explode in his arms.

My whole body goes tight and my toes curl as I press into his powerful chest. His arm is like rock, holding me up while I squirm, coming like a freight train. There's a keening sound, and it takes a couple of moments before I realize that it's me. It echoes off the walls, throwing the primal sound of my orgasm right back at me.

It's not until I begin to squeal and laugh as the tingling sensations become too much that he pulls the showerhead away. I let out a sigh of relief and go completely limp, his grip the only thing that keeps me from collapsing on the floor. Holy crap, that was intense.

"Warm enough yet?" He's still rock hard against me. I don't trust my voice, so I just nod, making him chuckle. "Good. I can only wait so long."

He drops the showerhead and it hits the floor with a loud clunk, spraying hot water wildly. Turning me around, he presses me up against the shower wall and mashes his lips against mine. His kiss is eager and possessive, claiming me while his hands boldly explore my body. His large cock is hard against my stomach, and unable to help myself, I slip my hands down to grip him, to feel his heat between my fingers.

The deep groan he makes when I touch him stokes the fire inside me. I stroke his length, sliding my hands up and down him, loving the silky smoothness of his skin. "I want you in me." The words slip out before I know what I'm saying. "No, wait." I look up at him as earnestly as I can, fearing rejection. "I want to try something." He looks at me curiously as I slide down to my knees. I glance up again to make sure I have his attention. "I've never done this before, so you'll have to show me, okay?"

He swells in my hand while he watches me, eyes bright and full lips parted. "Fucking hell, Angie. You're so perfect I almost don't care if it's real."

It hurts that he still doesn't trust me, but I push it aside for now. I don't trust him either, but I want this anyway. Licking my lips, I eye his cock with trepidation. I'm not even sure I can get my lips around it, but I'm going to try. I take him in, but just barely, stretching my jaw until it burns. Touching the underside with my tongue, I taste him for the first time. I explore his texture, sliding over his bumps and ridges. Somehow this feels dirtier than sex, even here in the shower.

He threads his hand through my hair and grips so tightly that it hurts a little. I look up with just my eyes and I'm a little scared by the intensity of his gaze. Then he pushes the back of my head, forcing me to take him deeper.

Oh God, I don't know what I'm doing. He bumps into the back of my mouth, and I struggle to keep my gag reflex under control. I brace against his thighs, trying to control the depth and he doesn't force the issue.

Instead, he uses his grip to teach me a rhythm, showing me how to move to make him feel good. For once, he's not making crude comments or trying to get a rise out of me. He's too busy moaning, the sound deep and sexy. His eyes are closed, so I can't help slipping a hand down between my legs. I'm soaked, and it's not from the shower.

His breathing comes faster, emphasized by sharp gasps. He thrusts, fucking my mouth while I tease him with my tongue. "Shit… I'm almost there, babe." Looking down at me hotly, he makes me blush when I realize he's watching me play with myself. His eyes are half-hooded with lust, and even his trademark smirk is gone as he tenses up.

I appreciate his warning, but if I'm going to do this, I'm doing it right. So instead of pulling off, I tighten my lips and swirl my tongue against him. Closing my eyes, I wait for it, not knowing exactly what to expect.

He lets out a deep groan and his thighs flex as he stiffens and swells. He comes hard, filling my mouth thickly before I swallow it down.

The shower wall rattles as he steadies himself, breathing heavily. I look up, and for the first time in the light of day, I see him without his mask on, his eyes closed and his face slack and vulnerable. When we had sex on our wedding night, it was too dark and I was too caught up in the moment to notice. I like it. It's like seeing into parts of him that he normally hides away.

I'm not sure when the right point is to stop, so I keep sucking. He twitches and laughs softly, obviously sensitive and maybe a little ticklish. As he softens, I discover I can take more of him in, and I do, exploring him with my tongue and lips.

Eventually, he pulls away. "Fuck, too sensitive."

I let him out with a soft pop before I look up, unable to keep the grin off my face. I did pretty well, I think, especially for my first time.

He laughs. "Feeling pretty proud of yourself, aren't you." Crouching, gets right up close. "You suck great cock, babe."

"Don't call me—"

He kisses me, deeply, putting a hand on the back of my head so I can't get away. Doesn't he care about… well, apparently not. I wrap my arms around his neck, and return his kiss for all I'm worth.

31 GAVIN

Well, fuck, that was unexpected. Far be it from me to not enjoy a spontaneous BJ, but I'm waiting for the other shoe to drop. Pretty sure I'm not out of the shithouse yet. I can't deny that our chemistry is real, but aside from my cock, what else is she after?

Even still, somehow I've ended up in bed with her head on my chest and my arm around her like we actually belong in the fucking bridal suite, and for once, I have no idea what to say. She sure feels good in my arms though.

She even smells good. I resist the urge to lean in and kiss the top of her head. Jesus. I never thought I'd end up like my father, but here I am pushing aside my pride because her mouth felt good around my cock and her hair smells nice. I blame the shower on adrenaline, but the cuddling?

Shit, now what?

"Nothing's changed, has it?" Angie's soft voice breaks the silence with a question that sounds more like a statement. Her soft breath brushes over my midsection while she traces the tattoo on my side with her finger. One of the first ones I got. A bunch of feathers wrapped in barbed wire. It seemed really fucking symbolic of... I can't even remember.

I sigh and look up at the ceiling, wondering about the shitty paint job. "No."

"I can't stop thinking about you." Her finger trails higher, up towards my chest, following black ink while she talks.

Cold settles in my gut. She's betting on my ego to get me back. Typical.

"And I hate it. I hate that you were a total asshole to me when I was scared and I still can't stop."

With a quick grab and roll, I put her under me. Angie squeaks in protest at the sudden movement, but I don't miss how her legs slide open automatically so I land between them. Her tits jiggle enticingly when she lands on her back, and I'm already hard just looking at her.

"Like hell you hate it." I grind my cock against her and she whimpers. "And scared? Scared of what? Being set for life? Oh yeah, poor you." I try to sound pissed, but man, it's hard when I can feel her heat soaking into me. I don't even believe me.

She frowns and tries weakly to buck me off, but she's breathing heavy and it's not from the effort. "Set for life? Are you serious? Yeah, I'd just looove to be pregnant for pre-med. Raising a baby on my own in medical school sounds like so much fun! And I'd be stuck with YOU which would basically be hell. I've been trying to get away from you since we met!"

I laugh. "Of course you have. That's why we keep ending up in bed together. You have to rest from all that *running*." I don't believe for a minute that she doesn't want to be exactly where she is. The rest of it? I don't know, but doubt creeps in. "I still don't know what to do with you."

"Really?" She traces her fingernails along my chest, sending tingles racing straight down to my cock. "The great and mighty playboy is out of ideas? How disappointing. I can think of a couple of things."

"Yeah?" Is this really the same girl?

"Yeah, like you get the fuck off me and we finish this trip and then never see each other again," she snaps.

"That'll be a little hard, *Sis*."

Angie laughs. "Didn't you hear? The marriage is off. Your dad pulled the plug."

The feel of her under me is so distracting that her words take a moment to register. "What? What do you mean?" I grab her hands and pin them to the pillow behind her head. From the way she chews her lip and her eyes light up, she doesn't look like she minds. "Spill."

"Mom told me." She raises an eyebrow. "Your dad hasn't called?"

"Apparently we don't talk as often as you guys do." As in, hardly ever if we don't have to. This would've been nice to know, though. "Tell me what happened."

"Why do you care? According to you we're just a bunch of gold diggers anyway. I can see it in your eyes whenever you look at me like that." She wriggles against my grip.

"Like what?" I ease up and sit back. The sexual tension between us just up and evaporated.

"Like I stop being a person and I start being a threat. Like you did yesterday, right before you called me names and stormed out on me. Are you going to do that again?" Pulling the sheets up, she covers herself. "Because if you are, can you just skip to the part where you leave?"

If it wasn't obvious already, playtime's over. How did we go from soft and sexy to being at each other's throats again in under a minute? I sigh. "Just tell me what fucking happened."

She blows her hair out of her eyes. "Someone from your dad's company invested in Mom's store. She thought it was him, being all super-secret philanthropist in love."

Shit.

"Well he wasn't, and when he found out about the money, he was pissed. He thinks she tried to scam him, to use him to save her business. Wouldn't listen to a word Mom said." She looks right at me, her brown eyes darkening. "Sound like someone you know?"

Fuck. My mind's racing. No good deed goes

unpunished. Boom, right back in my face. Angie's going to be furious.

Double fuck.

"It was me."

She's looking out the window, but her eyes snap to me at my words. "Excuse me?"

"I sent the money. Nobody was supposed to know."

Her eyes go huge before they narrow, her brows furrowing angrily. "You set up my mom?"

"No! I knew her stupid flower shop was in trouble, so I had one of dad's companies invest. I have a bit of clout in the company, even if most of the time he thinks my office is a waste of space. It wasn't a lot. Just enough to keep her afloat for a bit. I didn't want money to be an issue." I shrug. "For what it's worth, I'm impressed she figured out the connection."

"You are…" Angie sits up on the bed and clutches the sheets, not out of modesty but anger. "…the most paranoid, egotistical…" Kneeling up on the bed, she points at the door, an image of beautiful, stark naked fury. "…manipulative prick I know." Her heavy breathing makes her tits heave in a way that's ridiculously distracting.

I tear my eyes away to meet her icy gaze. I've done a lot of things I'm not proud of, but this was supposed to be one of the good things. "I was trying to help, for Christ's sake."

"Giving money as a freaking test isn't helping, dimwit. What, it wasn't enough to screw up what we had before we even had a chance? You had to go ruin it for our parents too?" She picks up a pillow and flings it at me which I only barely bat out of the way. Arguing while naked isn't playing fair. Not when you look like Angie.

Alright, I'm done with this. I can't win. "You know what? Fuck this. I'm leaving. I'll ask for another cabin for the rest of the cruise. You win. Happy?" I talk while I pull dry clothes out of my suitcase. She huffs, still naked and in full view, watching me pick up my stuff.

Does that make me hard? Of course it does, but I ignore it. I'll get my own cabin, jerk off and I won't even have to worry about her walking in on me. Fucking magnificent. I tug the zippers shut on my suitcase and open the door. With a last glance back, I meet her steely gaze with one of my own. "Have a nice fucking cruise." Then I step out, closing the door behind me.

Done.

32 ANGIE

I shift on the deck chair, finding a better angle for reading. A sip of sangria, then back to rippling chests and heaving bosoms. Funny how the reality of muscle bound alpha males never seems to match up with the fantasy. It'd be nice if every time I picture the hero in this story, he didn't look like Gavin.

I haven't talked to him in three days. The storm raged on for most of the day we fought, and then blew out overnight. Since then I've been living in paradise, and hating every second of it. I got what I wanted, so I should be happy. Pleased. Thrilled. I have an amazing suite to myself, a magnificent view, a huge bed, and best of all, I don't have a hotshot asshole of a stepbrother running around cracking jokes and trying to get in my panties.

Whoopde-freakin-do.

It's given me plenty of time to work on my tan, and while I'll never make a serious dent in my to-be-read pile, I've made the best progress in months. Just me, my e-reader, the blazing sun and sangrias. Perfect.

And lonely. I spend my days in imaginary worlds and my nights ignoring how empty my bed feels. If the storm hadn't knocked out the cell antenna it might not be so bad, but I can't even get in touch with Cassie or Mom. It's enough to make me miss Gavin's paranoia and asshattery. Not really. But I do miss his smile, and the way he sometimes looked at me before it all fell apart.

With a sigh, I put the reader down and roll onto my back, closing my eyes to the bright sun on my face. I've seen him around, of course. The ship isn't *that* big. Usually he's just wearing a pair of board shorts and a smile, showing off his bronzed chest and tattoos. Either a lot of the passengers didn't catch the whole wedding thing, or he's really going out of his way to show that it's not a problem, because I every time I see him he has a new girl on his arm. Or arms. I bet it took him all of an hour to replace me.

Fuck him. I'm sure those girls are.

I hate that I'm weak enough to be jealous, and that I'm still thinking about him.

Even with my eyes shut, I sense the shadow passing in front of me, blocking the sun for a moment. I open them immediately, expecting Gavin. I'm not sure why I thought it'd be him, but it turns out to be Joyce, leading Mabel to one of the deck chairs.

"Right over here, Mabel. Here are two chairs for us." She might be a little batty, but the love she has for her friend is plain in her voice. I wonder if Cassie and I will be like that when we're old. Looking at them, I smile a little. I could do a lot worse than cruising around and speaking my mind.

Joyce settles Mabel on the chair, giving her a hand when she sits down. "There you go. I'll go get drinks." She gives me a wave and a smile before heading to the snack bar. I peek over at Mabel, who looks after her with a sweet smile. Maybe they're more than friends? I grin at the thought. Never too old for love, I guess. Maybe there's hope for me yet.

I lean back, close my eyes and soak up the sun.

"You seem to be taking it well." Joyce is back,

and I'm assuming she's talking to me. Opening one eye half-way, I peer in her direction to find her examining me, her eyes crinkled tightly at the corners. "I've had some short affairs, but I'm pretty sure I never had a marriage that didn't last a day." Her face is full of sympathy.

How much do I tell her? "It's complicated."

"It always is, dearie, otherwise it wouldn't hurt so much." She looks at me expectantly, her open eyes and slight curves at the corners of her lips saying, "Of course you're going to tell me everything."

Then it all just pours out of me, and I mean ALL. The night at the club, Paul, our parents' marriage, the cruise, our marriage, our fights, everything. Once I start, I can't stop until I've unloaded, and through it all she listens silently. If her sparkling blue eyes didn't look so alert, I'd think she'd lost me long ago.

"So now, I guess he's got his own room somewhere. I've seen him here and there, but we haven't spoken since he left our suite." I study the deck intently after finishing my story, afraid to look up at her. It's pretty wild, and I'm just waiting for her condemnation. Stealing, lies, sort of cheating, sleeping with my stepbrother. Putting it all out there, it sounds like a soap opera.

"That is quite a tale," she chuckles.

"You don't think I'm horrible?" I dare to look, expecting the worst. "He might end up being my stepbrother!"

Joyce doesn't look horrified. She looks amused. "Stepbrother? That's nothing." She gathers herself. "I grew up in a small town in the middle of nowhere. I very nearly married my second cousin for my first husband, and some of the other girls weren't nearly that picky, if you know what I mean." Then she does laugh, bubbly peals of laughter tumbling out of her. "Trust me, dearie, it's nothing. You two aren't even related."

I laugh at myself. Getting everything out into the open makes me feel a little better. "I suppose you're right. Compared to how much of an assho— jerk he is, the step thing is nothing."

"All men are assholes sometimes." She laughs at the shock on my face. "And all women can be bitches given the chance. Or are you an angel sent down from heaven?" Joyce raises a perfectly lined eyebrow.

Be the bulldog, not the bitch.

I blush. "I don't know how to fix it. I don't even know if I *should* fix it. What do I do?" I guess it'd be too much to hope that the old woman has the answer.

"Does he still make you tingle, even when you're seeing red and ready to hang his walnuts up for the squirrels?"

"Joyce!" I laugh and blush even harder.

"I'll take that as a yes. I've felt that way about a man exactly four times." Her grin is sly, like she's waiting for me to make a connection.

"And you were married how many times?" I see where she's going with this, but just to be sure.

"Exactly, dear." She chuckles. "You're so much like me when I was your age, except they'd never have let us wear tiny bathing suits like yours." She gazes out over the ocean, lost in thought for a moment. "I absolutely could have, just so that's clear. I was lovely back then."

I laugh at the certainty in her voice. It was not a matter to be debated, obviously. "I'm sure you were. I bet you had the guys falling at your feet no matter how you dressed."

She purses her lips, looking unamused. "Are you teasing me, young lady?"

"Absolutely not." Hopefully, my smile looks friendly as intended and not patronizing.

Her lips stay tight a moment longer, as if she's weighing my response. Apparently it's good enough, since her smile returns. "In that case, do you really want to live the rest of your life wondering what might have been?" She eases back onto her deck chair and pulls her hat into her eyes. "Think about it. Life's too short. Trust me."

"Did you ever regret it?" I ask quietly.

"My husbands?"

I nod.

"There were times I had my doubts, but looking back?" Her wrinkled face goes soft and distant. "Not a moment, even the bad ones." She looks like she wants to be alone with the memories, so I turn to my own thoughts.

I feel a little more resolved to work something out with Gavin, but what? Marry him? I already tried that and it didn't really work out. Blowing the hair out of my eyes, I lean back into the deck chair and close my eyes.

One of us is going to have to make the first move, but will it be me?

33 GAVIN

I'm the shark, not the minnow, but someone forgot to tell these fancy-ass bitches that. Somehow word's gotten out that my sham of a marriage is in trouble, and now I'm practically holding fucking auditions for the next Mrs. Caldwell. The girls won't leave me the hell alone. In the bar, on deck. Hell, one actually knocked on the door to my room last night. It'd be fucking nice some days to not be a Caldwell.

I've barely thought the thought when a bleach blonde with balloon tits crammed into a skimpy red bikini slides onto the stool next to me, orders one of those chick drinks with an umbrella and a long straw. She sucks on it like it's a cock, while she grins mischievously and looks at me through her long eyelashes.

I make a point of turning my back to her while I sip my scotch. What's wrong with me? Only a few weeks ago, I would've been all over that. Drag her to my suite, fuck her silly and that's it. No strings, no obligations. Just fucking. Hit it and quit it. Buy her a little something nice, like maybe a top that actually fits, and she'd be happy as a clam.

Now? I'm not even fucking interested.

Apparently my cold shoulder's obvious enough, since the blonde stomps away with her drink, probably looking for someone who'll play her games.

It's all Angie's fault. She broke me.

For the first time, someone made me work for it. And the biggest fucking joke? When I thought I won, turns out I lost. She won, because she's out there enjoying herself and I'm in here with my brain stuck on the one woman who wants nothing to do with me.

It's like I wake up, think of Angie, jerk off, take a shower, think of Angie, jerk off, go out, think of Angie, and while I don't jerk off, I think about going back to my suite to take care of business. Because she's in under my fucking skin.

And not only is she having the time of her life

without me. She's going places. Fucking med school. What am I doing? Drinking. Go me. Maybe I should've stuck it out in business school. If Dad were here he'd be on my case and shouting "I told you so."

Speaking of Dad, I make another attempt to call out and fix the shitstorm I accidentally threw Marie into. I've been trying since Angie told me about it, but the connection has been down since the storm. I tap his picture and surprisingly enough the call goes out. Even more surprisingly, he picks up.

"What do you want?"

Great. He'd better fucking appreciate this. "Hi to you too, Dad."

"Where the hell are you? I haven't seen you since last week. Ever thought about showing up for work for a change?" Well, can't say he doesn't get straight to the point.

"You'd never believe it, Dad. I'm on a cruise. Isn't that amazing?" I put a little extra cheer in my voice just to piss him off.

I'm a bit surprised when he laughs. "You took those tickets? What would you do that for? Did you bring a date?" He's drinking something, and slurps it loudly, probably just to irritate me.

"Yeah, Dad. I did. I'm here with my shiny new sister. And good thing too, because wouldn't it have been awkward to go stag to my own wedding. Angie made quite the blushing bride."

The sound of him coughing as whatever he's drinking catches in his throat makes my day. "You went through with *my* wedding? Hope you got my money's worth. Just tell me I don't need to get my lawyers involved."

"Nah, we took off before he made us sign anything and trust me, nobody is expecting us to make it final now. But this isn't about my fucked up pretend marriage, it's about yours. It's about the money that went to Marie's flower shop."

"Who told you about that?" He listens, letting out his breath slowly in a deep sigh as I explain. "What the hell were you thinking? Do you know how bad you made her look? How bad you made *me* look?"

"Yeah, you know what? I'd give you a lecture about being a paranoid fuck and too suspicious for your own good, but I'll wait and let Angie do it since she does it so much better. Maybe she learned it from her mom. You're in for a treat." I roll my eyes, and for a moment I get a glimpse into how she sees me. "But yeah, Marie didn't know anything about it, so don't blame her."

"Oh, I won't. I'll blame you. You do some of the stupidest fucking things, you know that? When are you going to grow up, Gavin?" He's on a roll now. This is his favorite topic, how useless I am. "Speaking of Angie, you could do a hell of a lot worse than her. She works hard, she has goals, she reads. Books, Gavin. With words. You should try one some time."

"She hates my fucking guts right now, but good to know you approve. I didn't know all I had to do to impress you was to be literate. Maybe I'll try one of these 'books' you speak of." He can't see my air quotes, but I'm sure he hears them in my voice.

"Gavin…" he sighs. "You're too smart to keep playing dumb forever. One of these days you're going to find something you care about. I just hope it happens before you fuck things up beyond repair."

I could be wrong, but he almost sounds paternal. Maybe it's the scotch. "What can I say? Like father like son. If you fix things with Marie, maybe there's hope for me yet." It's weird. Despite it all, I think this is the closest we've had to real conversation in years.

He laughs. "I think we'd get along a lot better if we weren't so damned alike, Son." He pauses for a moment, weighing his words. "Thanks. Not for fucking up, but for letting me know. It sounds like I have some groveling to do."

Yeah. Me too.

He hangs up without saying goodbye.

Are we really that alike? Suspicious, judgmental, quick to anger. Fuck. Guess I've learned from the best. I've spent so long running from what my father wants me to be that I didn't even notice I was turning into him.

I don't want to be that guy, but I'm not sure I know how to be anyone else.

Angie would tell it to me straight. She'd laugh and poke fun, but I've seen her talk about the people she cares about. She's fucking loyal, and I could've had that. Instead I spit on it because I was too weak to deal with what it would mean if she was what she seemed to be.

Perfect. In a bitchy, sarcastic sort of way, but I'd get sick of anything else. I grin.

Perfect for me.

I drove her away, and I wasn't lying. She

probably hates me, but I have one thing working in my favor. The last of my scotch slides smoothly down my throat, and this time I don't motion for another. I know where she is, and she's not going anywhere until this cruise is over.

Time for plan B. Whatever the fuck that is.

34 ANGIE

A loud thrum that doesn't sound like typical engine noise invades the room. Is that a helicopter? Every time we heard one when I was little, my mother used to point it out and tell me to wave because it might be Daddy. I stopped waving long before he crashed, but I never stopped looking. Except now I look up and say a little prayer for the pilot when I see one.

I go out onto the balcony to look, just barely catching the blur of rotors from around the back of the ship. If I lean a bit over the rail I can see the tail as it swings around to land. I guess there's a pad back there. Hopefully nobody's sick.

The weather's gorgeous though, so I push aside my melancholy thoughts and duck inside to put on my bikini and cover myself in sunblock. I haven't run into Gavin yet since my talk with Joyce, but I'm hoping to get a chance to talk to him. I got a call from Mom last night letting me know everything was alright with her and *Herbie* again. Gavin must have talked to his dad, and no matter what happens with the two of us, I'm glad he manned up and fixed things with our parents.

I'm such a chicken. I should do the mature thing and find him, but I went to him last time. If he cared at all, he'd come to me this time, right? I refuse to chase him around the ship like I'm desperate for his attention.

Because I'm not. My life was just fine before he exploded into it and I'll pick up the pieces again if I have to, but some wounds take longer to heal than others. I don't know how he managed it, but the ache in my heart goes deep.

I've only barely gotten back outside on my balcony and settled on a lounge chair when the helicopter takes off again. This time I get a decent look. It's totally black and looks like something out of a James Bond movie, except the logo on the body looks awfully familiar. *Caldwell?* My stomach twists.

Did Gavin leave? Did he tell his father about the tickets and I'm about to get in huge trouble?

Oh shit.

I sit up and start to panic, not sure which situation is worse. That Gavin is so mad, or cares so little that he'd actually just leave, or that I'm about to be put in ship jail. Do ships have jails? The room phone rings and just about stops my heart.

OhGodOhGodOhGod.

"Hello?" My fingers barely touch the receiver, as if it might turn around and bite me.

"Mrs. Caldwell? Marie?" That name is haunting me, but if they are still calling me Marie, then they don't know I'm faking it, right? Please be right.

"Yes, who's this?"

The man on the other end laughs briefly. "It's me, Captain Chuck. Don't you recognize me? I'm hurt, well and truly, dear lady."

I giggle nervously. "Of course, Chuck. I'm sorry. The sound is pretty fuzzy on my end, and I didn't expect anyone to call. I'm sorry."

"Not at all, Marie. I'll have someone check the lines later."

Great, now I feel guilty about giving someone

extra work. "What's going on?"

He hesitates. "We have... a bit of a situation down here."

"Situation?" Panic pokes up its ugly head again.

"One that requires your presence immediately."

Is this another one of the things that Gavin's dad set up? Like the wedding wasn't bad enough? "Are you sure I need to be there? I have no idea what this is about."

"I'm afraid you do. I've already sent a steward to your room to fetch you. I think once you're here you'll agree that it was worth the bother." I can almost hear his grin through the phone.

Fool me once, shame on you, fool me twice... "Do I need to wear anything special? Fancy dress or anything?" Call me suspicious, but getting married in my swimsuit has made me a little cautious about surprises.

"No, no need. Just come as you are."

"Okay, thank you. I'll wait for the steward."

Sorry, Chuck. One evening of underdressed fun is enough for me. I throw on a sundress over my suit and give my hair a quick check. There isn't time for anything else before the steward is knocking at the door.

It's the same kid from the other morning, the one who hadn't been able to keep his eyes off my chest when he came for our wakeup call. He looks a little disappointed, probably because I'm not hanging out of my shirt.

"Right this way, Mrs. Caldwell."

He leads me to the elevator and we ride down in silence. It feels a little awkward, but it's not like we have anything to say to each other. He's just doing his job. It's not his fault if I'm about to walk the plank. Leading the way through a stately section of the ship I haven't seen yet, he finally stops in front of large shut double doors. The sign says LIBRARY LOUNGE. "Here you are, Mrs. Caldwell. The captain told me to tell you to go in, and that um… you won't be disturbed."

I nod, eyes wide. That sounds ominous.

35 ANGIE

Putting my hand on the doorknob, I twist and open.

The ship's library isn't large, but when I enter the room, I can almost believe that I'm walking into an old-fashioned study. No fireplace, but the walls are lined with heavy wooden bookshelves and dark green textured wallpaper on what I can see of the walls. The carpet is plush and looks soft. It's the kind of room that would make someone want to fire up a cigar or pipe if it weren't for the NO SMOKING signs.

In the center of the room are several deep leather chairs. They look both comfortable and impressive, in a faux-antique sort of way. Sitting there in a perfectly tailored suit and looking for all the world like he actually belongs in a library, is Gavin. He stands up as soon as I enter, the suit emphasizing his broad shoulders and the powerful V form of his torso. He looks so good that I almost forget to wonder why he's here, or why I'm here for that matter.

His face is unreadable. Is he nervous? That's not like him. His usual smirk is hidden, but the corners of his mouth turn up slightly as I enter. It looks more uncertain than cocky. What isn't uncertain is that he's glad to see me, and that I'm happy I took a second to get ready before I came. His hungry gaze travels over me, and warmth spreads downwards with a familiar tingle.

"Hi." Such a short word, and yet there's so much in his tone and the way he looks at me. He comes a step closer, then stops and pulls a bouquet of roses out from behind the chair. They're gorgeous, a dozen shades of red, no two alike, and their clear, sweet smell reaching me even from across the room.

"Hi yourself." My eyes dart from his face, to the flowers and back. "What's going on?"

My heart feels like it's on the top of a seesaw. I want to believe in the fantasy that this is a big romantic apology, but this is *Gavin* we're talking about. It's probably something his Dad set up for my mother. If I let myself believe too much, it will hurt that much more when I land.

I jump when I hear the click of the door closing behind me. A second click is the sound of the lock being turned. I don't know what I'm scared of, but being locked in makes me nervous.

The fear must have shown on my face, since Gavin's quick to say something. "Don't worry. It still opens from the inside. He's just giving us privacy."

"Privacy for what?" If I didn't know better, I'd feel like I was being set up for a marriage proposal on one of those hidden camera shows, but that'd be crazy. We already had the wedding. A romantic proposal now wouldn't make any sense. If he gets down on one knee, I'm not waiting to find out, I'm running.

He stops an arm's length in front of me, but no kneeling. "Alright, this is probably going to be crap. Just bear with me, alright?"

I nod, curious and terrified.

"Angie, I'm sorry. I fucked up." He holds the flowers out, expecting me to take them.

I blink, caught off guard by the no strings attached honesty in his voice. There's not even a hint of arrogance or condescension. As if on autopilot, I take the flowers and hold them close, inhaling their sweet scent. What is he up to?

"The other day… Look, I accused you of some pretty shitty things. I'm sorry." It's like it's a word that he doesn't have much experience forming with his mouth, and he has to concentrate to get it out. "I can't promise I won't fuck everything up again. I probably will, actually. But can you give me the chance to try? If words don't convince you, I am willing to dedicate my tongue to a more passionate solution."

There's the smirk. I knew it couldn't hide for long. Only Gavin could turn a romantic apology into a proposition for sex, but it's so totally him that I can't quite keep a little smile from forming on my face.

He holds up a hand like he just remembers something. "Wait, I got you something else too. Call it a peace offering." He picks up a boxy package in brown paper with a pretty green bow from a low table near the chairs. "I think you'll like it."

Looking around, I try to figure out where to put the roses. Apparently, he's thought of that too, since he pulls a vase from a bookshelf next to him. I arch my eyebrow at him in surprise and he laughs. "Don't look at me. Captain Chuck suggested it. He's smarter than he looks."

"Maybe he's just apologized to more women," I joke.

"Maybe." Gavin trades me the package for the flowers.

The brown wrapping is simple, but it feels like quality. The ribbon too, it's actual velvet and hand tied. No cheap drugstore bow with a square of sticky tape like usual. This is all probably normal for Gavin, but I've never held a gift that felt so opulent before. I look up at him while he sets the vase down on the low table. "What is this?"

"Open it and see."

For reasons I can't explain, my heart starts pounding rapidly, like it knows there's something special in there. I'm almost afraid to open it and find out, spoiling the magic. I force myself to take my time, untying the ribbon and carefully pulling the tape that holds the wrapping together. Inside is an unmarked box, and in it, another wrapper in softer paper, so thin that I see the outline of the present through it. It's a book, but…

I pull the wrapper aside and gasp. It's a book bound in leather. It looks ancient. Stamped into the cover is the title, "Alice's Adventures in Wonderland." By Lewis Carroll. Very gently, I open it, taking care not to damage the pages, marveling at the beautiful images and the pretty type.

"It's from the first print run. I think it might have been rebound at some point, but everything else is original. I figured you could use a book to start your fancy library with."

I hear his voice, but I barely absorb what he's saying while I leaf through the book. It's so beautiful. "Gavin…" I flip to the title page. 1865. He's not kidding. It must be worth a fortune. "This is amazing, but I can't take it. It's too much. And where did you get it?" As soon as I ask, I remember the helicopter. "Wait, *this* is what the helicopter was here for? You airlifted a book for me?"

"And the flowers. I wasn't exactly going to find what I was looking for between the postcards and the fridge magnets in the gift shop." His voice is smug, like what else would you do if you're trapped at sea and need a grand gesture? It doesn't hurt that he knows he nailed the gift just about perfectly.

Shaking, I carefully put the book back in its box and set it on the table next to the roses. "I'm afraid to touch it." I turn to face him and find him a lot closer than I expect. He looks like the cat that got the canary. "What if I break it?"

"Then we'll get another book, but you won't. Who else will take as good care of it?" Reaching out, he puts his finger under my chin and lifts, forcing me to look into his eyes. Suddenly, I'm out of breath, my heart thundering in my chest. He leans closer. "It's just paper. What are you afraid of?"

I tear away from him, turning my back. It's surprising how hard I find it. "Gavin, that paper is probably worth more than I am."

"Impossible." His breath is hot against the back of my neck. "What are you really afraid of?"

"You," I whisper. "You can't accuse me of using you to get things, and then give me things to fix it. How do I know you won't use it against me?"

"I guess you don't." His frank answer throws me off. "Forgive me or don't. I want you to have the book, either way. It's not a trade. I can't imagine that it could possibly be in any better hands than yours, and a trip as crazy as this one deserves something special as a reminder."

His hands close around my upper arms. "I can't stop thinking about you, babe, and I hope you're as sick of denying this thing between us as I am. I hope you like the book, but personally I couldn't give a fuck about it. What I was really hoping was that it would get your attention long enough for you to accept my apology, because that's what I need more than anything else right now. *You're* what I need more than anything else right now."

This whole setup is like out of a movie written specifically to make me fall in love with him. It's almost too perfect, and a little bit of the bitch slips out, trying to hurt him and make him show his true colors. "Run out of girls to pass your time with?"

His fingers go tight around my arms. "I didn't touch them. Not a single one. If you want to push me away, you're going to have to try harder than that. I don't expect you to trust me right away, but tell me what to do to fix this, and I will." He holds me closer. "All I can think about is you."

I want to believe him. No, I do believe that he means it, *now*, but what about tomorrow? Next week?

How can this work? "What about our parents?" I'm running out of reasons not to give in.

"What about them?"

"Don't you think it would be kind of awkward, *Bro?*"

There's a quiet pause before he laughs. "I called Dad, you know. To tell him about the money."

I'd assumed, but it was good to know. "What did he say?"

"That I'm an idiot, more or less. And that I could do a hell of a lot worse than you. To be honest, I kind of got the feeling he'd rather have you as a daughter than me as a son, but I'll try not to hold that against you." Gavin laughs humorlessly. "You're right, that would be awkward. But as far as not wanting us together? Be more afraid of him trying to lock you in before you can get away."

I let out a short giggle. "I'm not, you know."

"Hm?"

"Trying to get away."

He pulls me close, holding me tight against him. "Like you have a fucking choice. You're mine."

The intensity in his voice sends shivers down my spine. "So you think you've won, do you? What if I

319

change my mind?" From the way heat is pooling between my legs at his firm touch, I realize the question is very, very hypothetical.

He growls into my ear, "I really don't like to lose."

I break. It's a victory I'm happy to give him. Wrenching myself loose from his grip, I turn around and reach up around his neck with both hands. Sliding my fingers into his hair, I pull him down to me, and he comes eagerly.

36 ANGIE

Suddenly, it's like even my sundress is too hot. I can't imagine how he feels in his suit. I might have started the kiss, but Gavin's determined to finish it, cradling the back of my head with one hand and putting the other at the small of my back, pressing me against him. Even through his pants, his hardness presses against my stomach.

I forget where we are. The flowers, the book, nothing matters except the connection between us, the electricity that's arcing across our lips as we kiss. My hands roam over his hard body, looking for buttons and zippers and anything I can use to get his clothes off. His jacket falls, and I fumble with his shirt, only pausing so he can lift my dress over my head.

Finally his last button gives and I spread his shirt open, revealing the smooth, muscular chest underneath. Leaning in, I kiss his nipples and all the skin in between while he works his sleeves down his arms before throwing the shirt aside. The salty taste of his skin mixes with the sweet scent of the roses next to us, creating a heady perfume.

I'm tearing open the fly of his pants when my bikini top goes slack, the knot undone by his clever fingers. Letting it slide down my arms, I toss it onto one of the chairs before I grab the hem of his pants and tear them down his legs, underwear and all as I drop to my knees. I'm rewarded by his large cock bouncing free only inches from my face, pointing straight up.

I don't even let him get his pants all the way off. Rising up, I envelop him in my mouth, trying to remember everything he taught me in the shower. His musk intoxicates and incites me. As I do my best to swallow him, all kinds of crazy, sexy tingles race up and down my skin.

He slides his hands into my hair, gripping me with hard fists and guiding me while I wrap my hand around the part of him that my mouth can't reach. He thrusts with need, but suddenly pulls away. "No, too much more and I'll come."

I look up with a grin. "Okay."

He laughs at my eagerness while he kicks off his shoes and pull his pants the rest of the way off. I watch him undressing hungrily. Out of all the gifts he's given me today, *this* might be my favorite. Nothing can top him, or the feeling of finally being able to call him mine. Tossing the pants aside, he aims his intense hazel eyes at me. They're so hungry it's a little scary.

In the blink of an eye, he's on me, picking me up and nearly throwing me on my back into one of the leather chairs. Making quick work of my bottoms, he tears them off so hard I hear fabric rip, but I don't care. He hovers over me, breathing hard, then flips my legs onto the arms of the chair so I'm spread wide open for him. My heart feels like it's about to burst out of my chest, but I'm ready for him. Whatever he wants to do.

Gavin's nostrils flare like a bull's, but instead of just driving into me, he lowers his face while he grabs my thighs with his strong hands, holding me open. At first he just kisses along the insides of my thighs and up over my mound, touching me with his lips everywhere but exactly where I want him. He flicks his tongue right around the edges, teasing me until I try to follow him with my hips to lure him to my center.

Instead, he tightens his grip on my thighs to keep me in place. "Good things come to those who wait, babe."

I nearly growl in frustration, my hands gripping the armrests so tightly my knuckles go white. Almost instinctively, I reply, "I'm not your babe."

He laughs. "Is my mouth about to eat your sweet pussy until you scream my name? Right now, you definitely are, babe. Stop denying it."

Oh my.

I start to respond, but then he swipes his broad tongue firmly right up between my folds and I forget why I cared.

He doesn't reply, his mouth is too busy, but the way his eyes crinkle into tight crow's feet shows how much he's smiling. Then I forget all about that too, closing my eyes and letting his tongue work its magic. He swirls, nibbles, kisses, blows, and basically pulls out every possible trick in the book until I'm a quivering mess beneath him, my whole body tightening up in anticipation.

I'm so, so close when he sits up that I whine in protest, making him chuckle. Tugging his discarded pants closer, he gets something out of the pocket. There's a tear of plastic and a moment of fiddling before he's back between my legs, but this time it's not his tongue pushing at my entrance. I draw a deep breath, waiting, my insides aching to be filled.

"You know, I think I might just be falling a little bit in love with you." He looks almost as surprised by his words as I am, but he doesn't take them back. His eyes bore into mine, like he's looking right into my soul. He's reading me like one of my books, and I don't even have to say anything. I can see that he knows.

Gavin pushes into me and my pent up breath rushes out in a long sigh. I'm so close that when he fills me, I shudder with the need to release, and when he leans in and takes my nipple in his mouth, I lose it. I come around him, clenching his thick cock, my toes curling and my back arching, pressing my breast eagerly towards him for more.

His big hands wrap around my waist, holding me in place as he fucks me, first with long, languid strokes, but then harder and harder until he's pounding me into the smooth leather chair. I grab onto him, my nails digging into his back and pulling him closer. Shaking with what feels like a storm of tiny orgasms in the wake of the big one, all I can do is cling to him and ride it out while I scream his name.

He fills me again and again, until he groans deeply and pushes all the way in. He swells, pulsing thickly while I hold him close. Long moments pass before we both relax, him gripping the chair for support and me slumping into it with a contented sigh.

We stare at each other, drenched in sweat and breathing like we've both run marathons. He's got a ridiculous grin on his face, and I'm sure mine's no better. I haven't felt this happy in a long time, and I want this moment to last forever.

It can't, of course, and I make sure to voice my protest when he pulls out. His cocky smile says it all. I'd be more disappointed, but I doubt it will be long before he's right back where I want him. Then he looks around the room. I follow his gaze and laugh.

Our clothes are everywhere, like a dresser exploded.

"I suppose we should clean up." Gavin chuckles while beginning to pick up. "I really like reading with you, though. Is it always that good?"

"Sometimes better." I curl up in the chair and watch him. "Some of the stories are *really* steamy."

He stops to arch an eyebrow at me. "We should definitely do some more reading, then. Now I'm curious. Up in your room?"

"Our room. Or are you planning on going back to yours?" I hope not. It's a big bed, and I've missed sleeping with him almost as much as I've missed the parts that didn't involve any sleep at all.

I admire the rippling of his back while he's pulling on his pants. The tattoos dance across his skin with his movements. It's hard to believe that all that is mine. I'm feeling possessive, and something tells me I'm going to be exploring and claiming every inch of that skin before the end of the cruise.

But first things first, where are my clothes?

My top I find shoved into the chair, and my dress was hanging off the table, but my bottoms are nowhere to be found. Gavin smacks my ass while I'm crouched over to look under things.

"Hey!"

He laughs. "Leave it. It'll make someone's library trip a little more interesting."

"I only packed one suit!"

"So I'll buy you new ones. Or better yet, keep you naked the rest of the trip."

I try to look scandalized, but I'm too happy to pull it off and he just reaches a hand up my dress to cup a bare cheek.

"Now let's get out of here so we can go take this shit back off."

Well, with an offer like that...

37 ANGIE

I curl away from the light peeking through our curtains, rolling right into Gavin's arms. His eyes are still closed, his breath even. I love watching him sleep, how his broad chest rises and falls and how his face relaxes. It's like seeing the real him, something he doesn't show very often, but that I'm not quite a stranger with anymore.

Running my fingers across his chest, I trace the lines and curves. Even with several days' opportunity to explore every inch of his body, I'm not tired of it. I don't think I'll ever be. I circle a nipple, and he starts to stir, at least a little bit. He looks at me through hooded eyes and smiles.

I roll onto him, straddling him so I can kiss him,

and almost regret it. "Ugh. Morning breath."

He laughs, waking quickly. "Right back atcha, babe."

It's funny how him calling me that doesn't bother me anymore. Guess it's all about who's saying it, and how. It used to sound condescending, but now it's different, softer. When I hear him say "babe", I also hear him whisper he loves me after he thinks I'm asleep.

I kiss him again. We can be gross together. If that's not love, what is?

His hands come around to clutch my ass. Something brushes against my thigh. He's waking up in more ways than one, and the evidence is hardening fast.

Patting his cheek, I grin at his eagerness. "Afraid not, champ. It's almost ten, and we're docking soon."

He groans in disappointment. "I'm sure they'll hold the ship for us."

I roll back off, grab a pillow and whack him with it. "Wakey wakey!"

He leaps into action, throwing the pillow across the room before rolling over me and pinning me to the bed. "I need my beauty sleep," he growls. His hard naked body over me makes me reconsider what needs to get docked where, and when.

Before I say anything, he climbs off. "Alright, dibs on the shower."

I pout but he's not watching. "Why not shower together?" The thought of seeing him under the water as it caresses the contours of his body and drips off him already has me wet.

"Because if we do, we're not getting out any faster than if we stay here and fuck." He grins and closes the door behind him. He even locks it, the bastard.

I hate it when he's right.

I almost jump him anyway when he comes out, but I'm a good girl. For now. I take my shower alone under protest. Soon after, we're dressed and riding the elevator downstairs to the lobby. We're packed in like sardines with everyone else getting ready to disembark. When we reach the main deck, we're of course in the back corner since we got on first and have to wait until everyone else is out. It's going to be a while.

"Time," he says.

"What?" I look around for a clock.

"The thing I want the most that I can't buy."

Oh, that. "Time?"

"Yeah. I used to think it was time with Dad." He shrugs.

"Why? I thought you guys couldn't stand each other."

He chuckles. "It's not that bad. He doesn't approve of most of the things I do, but I think he feels guilty too. He's running a multi-billion dollar corporation." With a sigh, he picks up his suitcase as the elevator clears. "That means not a lot of time for other things. Like your soon-to-be ex-wives. Or your somewhat unexpected son. So that's what I always wished for."

"That sucks." It feels lame, but I don't know what else to say.

"Yup," he agrees, then steps out of the elevator.

"Wait."

He turns, looking at me curiously.

"You said you used to think it was time with Dad. What is it now, then?"

That confident smirk that I used to hate spreads on his face. "Time with you, babe."

EPILOGUE

"Mr. Caldwell. Dr. Wilson." Four years later, Captain Chuck might be a little bit more gray and a have a couple more wrinkles, but other than that he looks just the same, immaculate in his white dress uniform. He'd laughed hard when we explained why we wanted to him to marry us. Again, as far as he knew.

I smile gently. "Not a doctor yet, Chuck."

"I'm sure it's just a matter of formality," he laughs.

"Sure. And four more years of med school. And years of internship." The path to being a doctor is long, but I've survived pre-med. What's ten more years, right?

I take a moment to glance out over the ocean.

It's a gorgeous day on the deck of the Golden Emperor of the Seas. When Gavin and I decided where we wanted to get married, there really wasn't any question. It was just too perfect.

This time our parents are here, and weird as our situation is to some people, they are happy for us. We've all had four years to adjust, I guess. We mostly find it funny to freak people out by talking about "our parents". Mom and Herb don't think it's nearly as amusing, but whatever. These days we're just a normal family, or as normal as billionaire mother/daughter father/son families get.

We even pulled a few strings and found Joyce and Mabel so we could invite them. If Chuck was amused, Joyce found the whole thing hilarious. Of course, she got the story when we were here the first time, but it only made her appreciate the irony more.

The music starts, and I have a flash of deja vu. Barring a few central people, the crowd's different, but it looks the same. The long red runner from the door to the ivy-covered arch at the end looks the same. Captain Chuck waiting for us at the end is the same. We start the same walk.

But it's also different. We're older, and we know

what we're doing this time. And this time we know we're in love.

Oh, and I'm wearing a dress.

I look up at Gavin, who's taking in the setting. It's amazing how he changed once he started talking to his dad. More specifically, when he quit working for him. Things were tense for a while, but they worked through it. Herb never said anything, but I think he figured Gavin would come back crawling.

Instead, Gavin took everything he'd learned from his father and used it to start an investment firm of his own, and while he isn't making billions, he's well on his way. It made him take himself more seriously, and he's got more respect from his father now than he ever did before. Suddenly they're equals.

Fortunately our first pregnancy scare was just that, a scare, but maybe it's time to change that? I'm in no hurry, but I can imagine Gavin with our own son or daughter. He says he'll never be as rich as his dad, because he spends so much time with me. One day that will be *us*. But he also says that's why he's already more successful, so I can live with that. Quite happily.

For the rest of our days.

ABOUT THE AUTHOR

Kim Linwood is a sucker for bad boys, billionaires and alpha males. If they're all three at once, that's even better. When she's not writing about romantic conflicts and witty dialogue, she's herding two growing boys (who are of course not bad) with her husband.

You can find Kim on the web at http://kimlinwood.com and if you're interested in hearing about new releases and promotions, you can sign up for her newsletter at http://kimlinwood.com/newsletter.

You can also find Kim on Facebook, where she loves to talk bad boys, romance and share news about new books or books she likes.